Menkaraa
The Maturation of Sarset

Khpra Senwosret

Bloomington, IN Milton Keynes, UK

authorHOUSE

AuthorHouse™
1663 Liberty Drive, Suite 200
Bloomington, IN 47403
www.authorhouse.com
Phone: 1-800-839-8640

AuthorHouse™ UK Ltd.
500 Avebury Boulevard
Central Milton Keynes, MK9 2BE
www.authorhouse.co.uk
Phone: 08001974150

First published by AuthorHouse 7/26/2006

ISBN: 1-4259-0872-1 (sc)

Printed in the United States of America
Bloomington, Indiana

This book is printed on acid-free paper.

ACKNOWLEDGEMENTS

I wish to thank first of all the ancestors who shoulders my life is built on. To my wife Sekai who fought with me through every chapter and did a great editing job. To my girl Che' who's eye for English is impeccable viva the revolution, to a Baltimore artist Nos who captured the image of Menkaraa so well, thanks to A-I the meanest tagger I've met you saw the vision of the work. My mom who always supports my endeavors and last but not least my children who inspire me each day to put words to my visions and continue the struggle. Hotep and Love Khpra

TABLE OF CONTENTS

EXORDIUM

Africa, she is a land that many people have looked upon as blighted and forgotten – she is a mystery and a wonder all in one breath. There are many misconceived ideas about her, some of which I would like to dispel. Firstly, Africa is a continent, not a country. In fact, it is the second largest continent (Asia being larger). To say you originate from Africa is quite a mouthful. Its landmass is eleven million, seven hundred thirty thousand square miles. In comparison, the United States is three million, six hundred eighty-eight thousand, and eight hundred and eighty-two square miles. You could fit all of the United States in the northern Sahara desert alone.

The massive geography of Africa alone is staggering. I stress this point so that you can truly grasp an idea of where the tale of Menkaraa unfolds. From north to south she is five thousand miles, from east to west, four thousand miles, and she straddles the equator making it the hottest continent. Africa hosts the longest river in the world, the great

Nile (Aur), which flows from south to north – four thousand and forty five miles, beginning as far south as Uganda, where the White Nile originates, meeting the Blue Nile from Ethiopia in the Sudan, and finally flowing north to the Mediterranean Sea. Africa is home to Mt. Kilimanjaro in Kenya – which is nineteen thousand, three hundred forty feet above sea level.

The world's greatest artifacts, the pyramids, the sphinx and the great works of Abu Simbel, to name a few, were created by the indigenous people of its land. Africa is home to thousands of species of animals and plant life, the terrain is desert, rain forest, green land, mountainous, tropical – to mention a few. The people, speak thousands of languages, dialects, and are a multitude of phenotypes, complexions and physical structures, which in and of its self is dizzying. Africa is truly a prize of a homeland, and can never be marginalized by rhetoric or distorted by the European's rendering of its history and place among the other regions in the world.

Africa houses abundant and fertile land for agriculture, with ample room for man and animals to cohabitate. It has by all accounts been proven to birth the origin of man – and countless other 'firsts' in the world. It was in Africa were the first evidence of man settling down near the fertile waters of the Aur and growing crops was recorded, elevating man from 'hunting and gathering' to agriculture and society building to survive. Before foreigners outside of her borders encroached upon her soil, she knew no unrelenting enemies. War did not rip whole villages apart and decimate lineages. Great leaders were able to step forth in time such as Rameses, Chaka, Makeda, Thutmoses III, Aspalta – raising some of the most envied societies known to man; it is such a period that this story is squeezed into.

Before the latter kings that many have heard of, a small kingdom south of the renowned Kemet (Egypt) was coming into prominence. The King was a wise benevolent leader who had learned to rule the kingdom from a succession of kings before him. He was just beginning to experience in his time the invasions of other countries into the outskirts of his land. You see, during this period, mixed blood and foreigners were not seen on the soil of Africa. The kingdoms of Ghana, Ethiopia, Sudan, Kemet, Taseti, all had seen hundreds of years of peace after they had staked out the boundaries of their perspective lands. These kingdoms did not attempt to conquer the vastness of the continent, because the need to possess everything was not a pervading idea in the consciousness of Africans.

Menkaure was the son of a king, and in 5200 b.c.e, Kemet was a great power on the earth. Menkaure ruled over Kemet, which was the length of the river Aur. A skillful diplomat, his southern neighbors supplied him with soldiers and craftsmen, expanding his power and resources. His awareness of the priest clans, which had always troubled the land, and his diplomatic relations with his surrounding kingdoms of the west and east, made his dynasty one of peace, until an ill-fated day when a roué priest named Apep tried to gain an advantage over the King, and seize the country for himself and his ilk. Unfortunately for Apep, he did not foresee that the creature he summoned had its own agenda.

Africans see misfortune as a way to learn lessons in life and to evolve. Thus the unfortunate scenario that turned Menkaure into a creature of blood, he sought to use as an opportunity to turn the kingdoms of the north and the Far East into rubble. Bak, his grand vizier, saw the coming trouble of these kingdoms and persuaded the King to wage an expansionist campaign, now that they possessed the interesting powers of Ausar, Kemet God of Resurrection. This backdrop is a discourse in the possibilities that many African kingdoms and clans faced as their homes and borders were encroached upon. Some Africans did not see expansion as a way to conduct themselves and their kingdoms. The world outside their borders they viewed as harsh and obsessive; there, new enemies wanted to destroy the African race. Menkaure's approach was visionary, and his grand vizier, Bak, understood that the reality of the insulated world that the many African kingdoms had experienced was now drawing to a swift close in the early pharaonic age.

By the time this tale unravels, Menkaure's youngest son, Menkaraa (men-kaw-raw), is faced with a world totally different than his youth, and the kingdom created by his royal linage had all but perished. The family curse weighed so heavily on his personage that he no longer looked at his surrounding country. He did not see the enemies of Africa crushing the land under their feet. He did not see, nor was he concerned with the suffering of the people or the city that he resided in. Menkaraa felt alone and loathsome – it would take a great movement of some proportion to attract and lure Menkaraa out of his isolation – and this is the beginning of the tale of Menkaraa.

.

CHAPTER ONE

It is nightfall in Karnak. You can hear the wind sweeping through the trees. The sound of broken shrubbery crackling under the scurrying about of night creatures is constant. The pouring rain is unrelenting, pushing and lunging itself toward the earth as the trees whistle and dance in rhythm to the melody of sounds. The sun has long retired into the night sky, and no creature dares to leave the safety of his or her enclave.

In the deep of the woods, a sound emanating from the house is that of a siren singing and humming, her melodic voice easing out of the walls and windows of a small structure. Youthful; her beauty is stunning, her statuesque form working a fire in a kitchen preparing a meal of beans and bread. Her hair black as the night sky is curly, thick, and resembling soft wool.

Her clothing clings tightly to her flesh. The neckline squeezing her full breast, pressing against them like water trapped in a dam. Her hips are full and softly rounded, and telegraphing its hidden treasure. She is unaware that she is being watched. The crack of thunder startles her. She blames her momentary uneasiness on the storm, and nervously continues humming and singing to ease her discomfort.

In the distance, a pair of eyes is watching. They belong to a being unseen in this region, but spoken of by old men telling tales in the village circle. Discreetly positioned within a line of trees nearest the kitchen window, the stranger is tall and straight like the trees, with broad shoulders, muscular arms and legs. He is wearing an ancient-like skirt made of fine linen, pleated softly from the waist, and clenching tightly to his hips. His bronze chest is fitted with a gold crossing bandoleer strap. His biceps flexing on contact at the pelting rain, his eyes remain fixed on the woman.

Mesmerized by her movements, he fixes his position on her while the rain splashes his chiseled face. His sharp incisor teeth creep out toward the edges of his mouth causing a tiny trickle of blood to appear. Usually a sign of hunger, he does not lust for her blood, for he could take her as prey like any living thing in the forest. His intentions are far from destroying her loveliness. The woman has stirred his emotions, and ensnarled his heart, something no other human has done before.

Menkaraa longs for her as he watches her bend and move about. Troubled as to how he should touch her, he knows that he could take her as he had done many times before, but this approach would not yield him the desired result. "Soon I will have you my sweet." He speaks determinedly to the forest, and quickly disappears into the cover of the woods.

Sarset turns and looks out the window, she notices movement among the trees, but her eyes turn up no evidence. She is a bit disquieted, but dismisses her uneasiness and returns to her chores. It is late and all that she can do this day is complete. She peeks into her parent's room, and is calmed to see them resting peacefully.

Lying in her bed, the fire from the hearth is crackling as if to replicate the easing storm outside her window. Sarset's mind drifts back to when she was twenty-one, and the evil ones came brandishing their sickle swords and childish book. It was a violent time. They destroyed her village, killed, and scattered her family and clansmen. Those days and nights of terror clung to her mind. She could not erase the horrific memory of the night they raided her village, killing fathers and sons, the old and young ones too weak to fight.

Sarset's mind races back in time. She and her parents are fleeing from a group of soldiers. As they made their way to the edge of the woods, it is apparent that they would be caught. The sun, already dying in the sky, she suddenly turns to see several soldiers bearing down on a tall mysterious stranger standing between their imminent capture, and the bloodthirsty soldiers. Seeing him from the back, she noticed his long locked hair falling at his shoulders his, broad muscular back blocking the last rays of the waning sun. Sarset knew he was not one of her people. She watched him, hidden by the bush.

The first soldier drew near. He tried to thrust his sword into the chest of the stranger, but he did not move. The Stranger grabbed the soldier by the throat, handling him like a rag doll; and tossing him twenty feet into the trunk of a tree, snapping his body in half upon impact. The other soldiers furious yet cautious, charged this time in pairs. As he sprang forward, a sword just seemed to appear in his hand, and with ease, he severed the heads of both soldiers in one fluid movement. The sword dripping with blood, clenched in his fist, the muscles in his forearm flexing, seemed to have a life of its own. The remaining soldiers did not stay long, and like cowards, took flight into the cover of the thick woods with the stranger pursuing them; the stranger's fighting skills overtook them quickly. Into the distance, their deafening screams could be heard.

Increasingly, Sarset's thoughts have been on the stranger that saved her that night arousing deep passions within her. She wondered who his people were, what village he came from, and why did he save them, and not hunt them down as he did the unfortunate soldiers. She was tired. Her thoughts about the mysterious savior carried her to sleep.

Menkaraa's strides are quick and deliberate as he moved toward his lair in the mountains. Once again, the beautiful one had delayed him from getting back to his home. Her beauty had stunned him, and therefore he had not hunted. By tomorrow, he would be starving. His mind wondered how he had become so taken by her.

He remembered that fateful night when he first saw her. Hurried footfalls racing toward the entrance of the forest, he was only 200 yards from the soldiers who were aggressively pursuing three bodies. Normally he would not interfere in the food chain business. However, as the sounds grew near him he saw a young woman making her way to the edge of the woods. Her long black hair swaying side to side, her loveliness he noticed instantly, and two other bodies struggling just behind her. He took great pleasure in destroying those foolish soldiers, like kenneling wood, one by one they fell before him. As usual, he wasted no time, and quickly ran the others down and drank their blood. Upon returning to the scene, the woman who had drawn him into the affair had disappeared into the cover of the woods. Although, disappointed, he knew it did not matter. He would find her at his appointed time.

CHAPTER TWO

Menkaraa's mind eased back to the present. His home is perched upon a peak in the line of mountains outside of Karnak. Observant eyes could notice the rough wrought stones, and door size windows from the bottom of the hillside. He looked around curiously and walked into a growth of bushes and dropped at least one hundred and fifty feet, and skillfully landed on his feet with a thud that would have shattered the bones of a normal man; nothing for this creature. Looking back up from where he fell, he mused at how the drop prevented the food from stumbling upon him. He open the massive stone door before him, he smiled at his strength and agility. A beautiful creature he was, and as for his physical strength, there was no equal.

His chamber suited its location; the walls are like the ancient tombs of Kemet, with Medu Neter and painted scenes of an ancient time inscribed on them. A large male lion stood attentive by a solid gold seat. The lion approaching him, nudged its huge head against his master's thigh. Menkaraa stroked his head. "Ku, I can see you missed me tonight?" A beautiful animal, the beast reminded him of the lions that guarded the great halls of his homeland in ancient Kemet. Menkaraa wondered how long it had been, one thousand years, two thousand or more since his exile. He no longer kept time, but Ku brought back fond memories of a time when his kind was worshipped as Gods.

Menkaraa sat down, stroking Ku's head. The lair was safe, a place away from the sun and humans. Adorned with relics from his past; the chair, in which he sat, was made of gold and trimmed with fine teak wood and could seat two people comfortably. Still dripping wet from his walk through the forest, his immortality made him immune from the ever-present chill of his underground chamber. His rain soaked locks, splashed on Ku - obviously annoying the beast – who showed his momentary displeasure by pawing at the wetness, and moving agitatedly to another spot in the room to rest. "You are acting like a child, have I spoiled you my friend?" Menkaraa was amused by his companion.

Menkaraa stood up, walked across the room to a finely crafted door and opened it. This was his sleep chamber, and in the room was a massive size bed meticulously dressed with beautiful silk and finely woven cotton coverings. Menkaraa did not sleep in a coffin like the vampires of the North. He came from a land and people who worshipped his kind as Gods, not reviled as the vampires of Europe had been for centuries. The worshiping did not last forever, the worshipping ceased, and the people no longer believed in his kind, and he was one of the few who escaped the massive death hunts. Over time, he learned to live with the curse passed down to him from his ancestors. His special abilities enabled him to outlive all those that despised and hated him. However, this was no consolation because he was left alone to deal with the pain of seeing all those he loved perish from this realm.

His mind snaps back to the present. This woman who has invaded his world; she is like the great Nefertari, Queen of Queens and Joint Ruler of Kemet. His feelings are confusing. What should he do, he thought. Should he give her the kiss, and make her his immortal lover? On the other hand, continue to agonize over her beauty from afar like a love sick human? Feeling weak from not hunting, his sleep lures him, he whispers "Sarset, my beloved" his eyes close shut.

Sarset's sleep is abruptly interrupted as she quickly rises from her bed. Was she dreaming, or did she hear her name being called? The sun was already creeping into her room, and she wonders if she has overslept. Sarset was beautiful in her waking state. Her long thick hair fell upon her soft caramel shoulders. Her breasts were full and pressed at her night clothes as if a lover had laid beside her and aroused her body awake.

Sarset headed toward the washbasin for her morning ritual. It was a delight for her to remove her nightclothes and take inventory of herself. Her face was nice, pleasant and shaped like a heart with no blemishes on it, except for a black mole situated near the corner of the left side of her mouth. She was flawless, teeth white as ivory, eye's dark as the African sky, nose full and button shaped. She was a natural beauty. Sarset splashed the cool water on her face; it felt invigorating to her skin, waking her otherwise sleepy face. She felt alive at this moment in spite of all the death she had witnessed. This simple morning ritual seemed to ease some of the pain of the past.

Sarset paused. Looking at her self in the small cracked mirror, tears began to race down her cheeks. She was quickly reminded by her emotions that she had not had the opportunity to have a lover in this life. She thought about the stranger in the woods. She wondered if he was betrothed or if he already had a wife and family. She quickly brushed off her thoughts and finished washing. She had important business to take care of in the market. She hated going there; it was unsafe and infested with evil ones only interested in doing harm to her type. She didn't want to be spotted by any of those evil men. In spite of the inherent danger of the journey, the needs of her parents were pressing and far more important than her own personal insecurities. She knew if she left early enough she would be home before dark, and usually the light of the day was enough to keep them in line. If it were not for her parents she would have abandoned this god-forsaken place, she thought, rubbing the last drop of oil on her smooth caramel skin.

Grabbing her satchel, she clutched the last pieces of gold hidden beneath a scantily filled pot of grain. Like this shelter they lived in, she never knew where the gold had come from. After being left homeless by the massive raids of the evil ones, she had stumbled upon their current cottage and has lived there ever since. She had always feared its rightful owners would return one day, but they never did. Like so many others, they too perished in the raids, or the fear of returning beckoned them to live somewhere else. They had been there for several days, and were nearly out of food, on their last meal of wild herbs and roots, when she saw this strangely crafted box filled with gold. She had combed the place for resources thoroughly, but had never come across the box. In her mind, she credited the ancestors for watching over them. She slipped the gold into a hidden compartment underneath her clothing.

Sarset intended to leave before the afternoon, but time had gone by quickly. Working her way through the woods, Sarset was tired and winded, hurrying her footsteps to make up for lost time. By the time she got to the market, it was near closing and she had already attracted the interest of some evil ones watching her exchange the gold pieces for supplies. Gold was not a typical currency in Karnak; most used bartering as a means of commerce. In an effort to avoid the evil ones, she disappeared in the alleyways while a young soldier made a commotion outside a tavern. Making her way through the small alleyways, she figured she could shake the soldiers if she stayed on the unfamiliar alleyways away from the main streets. Even though it took longer, she seemed to stay out of sight from her would be aggressors and located the opening to the woods leading back to the main path to her home. Quickening her pace, Sarset is worried that the evil ones are still interested in her. Not wanting to take any chances, she breaks into a sprint as she heads deep into the forest hoping to lose her pursuers in the thickness of the bush. Staying alert to danger, she cautiously but quickly makes her way through the forest. It was getting dark quickly, and she was unfamiliar with the woods at night. "Ancestors, I bid you to return me safely to my home," she whispered. The darkness continued to descend on the forest, and Sarset cursed her luck.

Menkaraa's door to his chamber slowly crept open; the ancient one had not awakened from his sleep completely, yet he sensed something was in his chamber. His eyes opened slowly, the face of Ku stared back at him. Upon seeing his master's eyes open, he began licking him on his face. Menkaraa admonished the beast; "You know you are not to enter my chamber before I awake my friend." He brushed Ku away with his arm as he stood to his feet. He was hungry, and like Ku, flesh was his meal.

He reached for his clothes, and dressed as only a vampire could. His movements were faster than a man or woman could follow with their eyes. It appeared as if he always had on clothes. Menkaraa was amazed at the things his body could do. Such as dissipate his form and appear as smoke, and then rematerialize. This took quite a bit of energy but he always recovered quickly. He learned from his childhood instructors how to make the molecules of his body change their structure so he could levitate – this was simple chemistry and physics. To men, they were gods walking upon the earth. Menkaraa patted the haunches of the lion as he fed him fresh deer flesh from the forest. He loved Ku; they were similar in so many ways.

Sarset was startled by the sounds of the woods at first, cautiously growing more accustomed to the noises of small animals rustling about in the bushes. She moved as quickly as she could, clutching tightly a medium size satchel containing herbs, dried milk, potatoes, flour, and oils. Instinctively she began to quicken her pace. Stopping briefly to confirm her suspicion, she could hear voices in the not too distant woods behind her. She was certain it was the soldiers that had spotted her in the market. She did not know their exact location, but she knew that they were almost on top of her.

Clutching her satchel tightly, she quickly bolted deeper into the forest. There were six of them, their feet brutalizing the ground as they pursued her. They intended to catch their victim, and had been plotting ever since they spotted her in the market. They knew their chance would come once she left the crowded market place, so they watched her as she made her way through the village in an attempt to lose them. The forest would shield them from the prying eyes of the villagers, even though they did not care about those black worms, but they did not want any more trouble than necessary. They paused for a moment, scanning to hear their prey moving or breathing. Sarset had stopped running, and was now crouched behind a cluster of bushes. Suddenly the group's leader shouted, "good she's stopped we can take her now." The leader stepped into the direction of the bush. Sarset dead still, clutched a stone in her delicate hands. The leader walked toward the bush and in one quick movement Sarset leaped toward him and struck him on his face with the stone.

"Ugh", he cried out – "get that bitch!" Sarset got up on her feet and tried to run but the other men quickly encircled her subduing her easily. Sarset screamed out but her voice seemed to disappear into the emptiness of the forest. The leader standing before her now, chest heaving, wiped the blood from his wound. "Cry out all you like, only the forest hears you." Leaning over her now exposed body, he backhanded her whipping her face and landing her against the harsh ground. Sarset was strong and she took the full impact of his hand, but she still mustered up enough fight to raise her head and spit in his bearded face before slipping into a daze. "You'll regret this you nasty little darkie."

Two of the men grabbed her on the ground, as she lay helpless the leader ripped at her dress, groping at her shapely form, laughing indignantly as he began to assault her body. "Before I kill you and take your gold, I'm going to get a piece of your dark meat." The other men seemed almost to be salivating like dogs at the thought of tearing into her flesh like animals. Just as the leader began to force his drunken lips onto her protruding breasts, "Enough", a voice commanded, booming from a distance. Sarset could not tell where the voice emanated from, she was slipping in and out of consciousness, but she knew it wasn't the voice of the ringleader, or one of his dogged men. She tried to push the stinking man off her, but only her imagination complied, her arms lay lifeless. They turned to see who had dared interrupt their deed, and standing approximately ten feet away was a tall, foreboding dark figure, seemingly to their eyes to be dropping from out of the trees.

Startled and agitated, the leader stepped forward. "I don't know where you come from my friend, but you have made a big mistake meddling in our business." Menkaraa smiled cruelly at the men. He

loved the moment before a fresh kill, especially just before he was about to decimate a loathsome being like this fool before him. Then he looked at the near naked woman lying before their feet, he spoke quickly and resolutely. "Understand, I'm not your friend, and when has ravaging a helpless woman become business." Suddenly he bore his incisor teeth at them like a leopard. The men stumbled back over the terrified body of Sarset at their feet, who was mumbling unintelligible words. Menkaraa lifted the arrogant leader by his collar and drew him to his mouth ripping his throat all in one motion. He screamed only for a second and was dead as Menkaraa dropped him to the ground like discarded trash. They stood there motionless as they watched their nemesis appear suspended for a moment while his body assimilated the blood of their leader. Menkaraa, regaining his senses, wiped the blood from the corners of his mouth and pointed his sword defiantly at the remaining men.

The men wasted no time, and fled into the woods like cowards, but it was too late, this was the blood frenzy, something that Menkaraa had grown accustomed to. It can only be described as the way you feel when you have gone too many hours without food and finally stop to eat. At this point, his vampire instincts were in full control and he was famished. Menkaraa first leaped and landed right in front of the men, cutting them off. His chest heaving, in between breaths, he spoke in

a monotone voice. "This night you have sought to assault a helpless female, with the same impunity I will assault you and send you to your fabled god." One of the men, warbled out, "Allah, help us," just before Menkaraa systematically devoured each of the pitiful humans. As the last meal fell to his feet, he turned to Sarset, barely standing, confused and disoriented, clutching pieces of her torn dress, her bare body revealed, staring at him in disbelief and horror.

He caught her just before she dropped to the ground like a sack of potatoes. Her long beautiful hair draped over his arm, her body fully exposed. Menkaraa was intoxicated by her loveliness. The blood dripping from his mouth released a droplet, which fell on her neck and raced down her bare breast finally resting at the tip of her nipple. It was enough to make him kiss her at that moment. His body was in control, and for a second, he opened his mouth wide, revealing his incisor teeth. He lowered his mouth to her lovely neck. He could smell the vanilla oil on her skin. In spite of her simple life and poverty, she paid attention to such a feminine detail. The smell reminded him of his mother. The scene of her loveliness jolted him back to reality releasing her neck from his mouth. He was intoxicated by her, but strangely he possessed a great love and respect for her life, however lonely and loathsome it had been. It dawned on him that he loved her life, as much as he loved her.

Gathering her in his arms, he was careful not to let the ground violate her body and placed pieces of her dress to cover her shapely curves and bare breasts. He knew he could not leave her here nor could he deliver her to her home. Right now, she needed care and rest, and he would provide this for her at his lair.

He levitated above the ground not wanting the forest to brush against her and began a careful ascension toward his lair. Approaching the covered opening to the great drop, he slowed his descent being careful and gentle with his load. As his feet touched the firm earth, Sarset lay limp in his arms, her breathing shallow, quick and disturbed. He pushed open the door. Ku immediately sprang toward him. Menkaraa merely looked at the beast and Ku, immediately turned away. "Not now my friend." Menkaraa was not going to place her in his resting sanctuary, so he made his way up the colonnade toward the castle he rarely used. The rooms were large and spacious there, more suitable for his special guest he thought.

Menkaraa never entertained in his vast home. It was merely kept to prevent the villagers and unwanted visitors from finding his sleeping lair. The door swung open and the room was quite beautiful compared to his somber room. Adored with a finely carved four-post queen size bed and a beautiful antique chest with fine carved Medu Neter

(hieroglyphs) on the face of each drawer. Menkaraa had them made many years ago by a craftsman he befriended in Benin.

He approached the bed and gently laid Sarset down. Her de-shuffled clothes caught his eye again – it took his breath away. Her lips were full and pouty like she had kissed in her sleep. Her hair all over her head now fell like waves on the pillow. Her soft shoulders and breastbone protruding out at just the right depth. Her carotid vein pulsating, stirred yet another sensation in his being. Her breasts were full and taunt, her nipples pushing out of her dress. A piece of her torn dress only slightly covered her hips, exposing her undergarments and the beauty of that spot finally made him turn away. He felt his vampire teeth etch their way out of his mouth and realizing he needed to step back; her lovely body would not be invaded like that, he thought. She would have to ask for his kiss and then he did not know if he could indulge her. He walked toward the door and closed it behind him. He worried about the impression he made with this woman. She saw him destroy those villains like a Serengeti lion attacking an antelope. What will she think when she awakes? Darkness would be slowly slipping away making room for the morning sun. It was time for him to sleep.

CHAPTER THREE

Sarset turned slowly, murmuring softly. Suddenly she bolted up opening her eyes; she had no idea where she was. Her eyes darted back and forth across the room, but nothing was familiar. "Where am I," she whispered. She touched her clothes and realized that her dress was torn and exposing her nakedness. The memory came rushing back. She drew in a breath, and placed her hand over her mouth. She wanted to cry, but no tears would flow or sound came out of her mouth. She thought about seeing those men ripped into pieces by the stranger, or beast so it seemed. She remembered the blood from the dead breaded man, and blood dripping from the stranger's mouth. How did she get here she thought, did the stranger bring her here, is he going to kill her as he did the others?

She adjusted her eyes to the room and noticed clothing laid out on the foot of the bed. Beautiful things made of silk and finely woven cotton. In the middle of the floor was a large gold tub; she was amazed at the size and beauty of it, and on the far wall, a fireplace warmed a container of water. She stood on her feet and walked over to the tub, which was partially filled with water. She skimmed her hand across the surface of the cool water. "Hello, hello is anyone there?" A growl at the door frightened her, "who's out there?" She buried her face into her hands as she crouched back down in a corner of the far edge of the room her mind racing trying to figure her situation out. She looks up, and at her feet, she noticed a small slip of paper, folded in half. She picked the note up on the note it read in neat cursive handwriting, you are safe my friend and your loved ones are being kept in the best possible manner.

Menkaraa had finished his mission for the evening. He had rushed the whole night to place some clothes out to prepare a bath and some food for her. Her parents did not seem to notice his peculiar manner and bearing. He explained she was visiting a friend after she left the market and because of the lateness of the hour decided to spend a night and return in a few days when it was safer to travel in the forest. Her parents were relieved she was safe and trusted his word. He introduced a young woman, whom he had paid with a satchel of gold to see after the old ones. He warned her that if any harm befell them, she would not live to regret it.

Back at his lair, Ku seemed agitated at the attention he was paying this room and the guest in it. Menkaraa petted and stroked him. "Watch after her my friend," as he made his way to his sleep chamber. Ku would keep her confined until he awoke the next evening. Menkaraa hoped she found all she needed. He hoped to speak to her soon and to find out more about this woman and where her heart lies. Ku growled in the distance, Menkaraa simply smiled and acknowledged his intelligence.

Sarset calmed her self. She was dirty and her clothes were destroyed. She had already conceded that she might as well take a bath, since whatever was at the door was not coming in, and not allowing her out. She still worried about her parents, but there was little she could do in her situation. She would just bathe and wait. She stood and peeled off her torn clothes. She carried the pail of hot water and poured it into the tub. It was very inviting as the steam of the colliding liquids combined. She unsnapped what was left of her undergarments and slipped into the water. The warm water was soothing to her body and nerves. Her mind was swirling with questions and why this was happening to her. This time the tears made their way out.

Sarset was still frightened, but admittedly now a bit curious. The room was so enchanting. Whoever lived here was quite wealthy and had great taste she thought. Near the foot of the bed, a small table was set up with fruit, bread and wine. Such care she had not seen except when she prepared food for her parents.

Her eyes moved back and forth over the warmth of the room, "what am I doing here?" she thought, as her cheeks were washed with tears. The hour, the day, she did not know. She felt okay, seemingly safe and the soldiers had done no real harm, except to her psyche. Her mind began to muse about the stranger, she knew he was something other than an ordinary man, that resplendent being she had dreamed of so many times. "Stop it Sarset", scolding herself, this stranger was something other than an ordinary man all right. She watched him decimate those men like a lion rendering an antelope for food, she wondered if she would ever see him again.

Menkaraa was stirring, he could feel the sun slipping from the sky, it was like his heart was in unison with its rising and falling. Rarely was he ever caught by the sun's appearance in the sky. He could be in the darkest place and unable to see the sun and knew its approach. Menkaraa was a rhythmic being, his walk, his movement, and his speech flowed in a predictable rhythm and ancient grace. The transformation from mortal to immortal had enhanced his entire human qualities ten fold. His eyesight enabled him to see over great distances of at least two hundred yards if there were no obstructions in front of him. His hearing if measurable would far exceed the ability of a wolf or domestic hunting dog. Words that humans spoke in a whisper he could hear as if they were shouting, if he locked his senses. His strength was not a simple thing to explain, because of his speed, his strength was limitless. Speed augments power and if he accelerated at a certain rate of speed with his hands and legs, he could navigate across a great chasm, or drive his partially indestructible body through solid stone.

Vampires are intellectually enhanced after their death as humans and coming back to animation. The blood of his father and that of his many victims bring with it their intellect. It is like having the minds of thousands of people and their intelligence at your beckoning. His hair was the one feature that he retained of human vanity. His father wore his hair like this, full and locked in the fashion of pre-dynastic warriors. His was full and grew like thick branches on a strong tree. Menkaraa preferred wearing his hair loose and hanging like a drape around his face.

He maintained his youth but beings such as him do not age like humans. Their life span is slowed metabolically. A fortunate vampire of one thousand years would appear to be in his early twenty's or beginning thirty's, depending on how well he fed and slept. He stood up and readied himself for the meeting of his venerable life. His hunger stirred in him. Would he have time to feed? His teeth pressed hard against the inside of his mouth, it was time to feed.

Sarset stepped out of the tub; her long lovely caramel legs were wet and glistening. They could easily drive any man wild with passion. She reached for the towels left out for her and began to dry her body. The towel seemed to be making love to her as she dried every inch of her body. In minutes she was done, and sitting in one of the magnificent chairs in the room. The furniture she was not familiar, it appeared to be from another era. It was lovely though, gold wrought metal, with a high back and wide seat similar to a chair for royalty. Sarset couldn't help but to notice the meal set at the table before her, she discovered how famished she actually was. She quickly wrapped her head with the towel, and slipped on the long silk gown, a deep rich purple with lovely lace sleeves and a low cut neckline revealing her ample cleavage. The fabric felt comforting against her skin, like a lover's caress. She momentarily reveled in the carnal pleasure it gave her. Such a beautiful garment had never graced her body before, she felt a little giddy, but the movement of something outside of her door interrupted the moment, and a low growl returned her to guarded.

He was quick, this pre-eternal being of the night. The first food that stumbled in his hunting ground he took, drank briskly and began to make his way back to his lair. Only an hour of his night had been used, and if you understand the mechanics of vampires, they treasure every moment of wakefulness. Humans can use twelve, fourteen, even sixteen hours of a day. The blood children have only ten hours more or less depending on the season and the area they live in. Menkarra planned to speak to this woman on this night until the sun approached.

Finally at his lair, he instinctively dropped the two hundred feet without a glance, had he hesitated just for a moment, like he usually did, he would have sensed the intruder in the trees. He pulled the stone door away and entered his lair. Ku jumped on him playfully, stroking his thick mane. "Have you kept watch over our guest, my friend?" He asked affectionately.

CHAPTER FOUR

Making his way through the tunneled underground passage, he thought of her and how he would introduce himself. As he arrived at the door, he found himself searching for ideas.

Sarset ate sparingly, but finished the food that she had picked from the tray and moved back to the large chair. She had bathed and eaten, and now was anxiously awaiting the moment when she would meet her host. The locked room thing was now a bit too much, and her concern about her parents was growing. Turning toward the door of her room, she thought she heard a voice. "Is someone there?" she whispered in a raspy voice. Reaching for her night covering, she slipped it on over her nightgown, her voice breaching the door, Menkaraa stepped back at first, he was at a loss for words. He quickly began picking up the questions in her mind.

He dematerialized in front of the door and reassembled himself in a dark part of the room. "The old ones are fine Sarset." She spun around to search for the place the voice came from. She could not see him. Menkaraa was still. He was best at stealth and he desired to watch her at first, as he had done it many times before in the woods away from her searching eyes. Her eyes were probing the room, "who's there?" She rose from her chair. "Be still sweet one," I wish only to look upon you and speak to you. The matter of your parents is being taken care of."

Sarset obeyed the voice in the dark and eased back down in the chair. She could not see the body that contained the voice in the shadow. "Sir, do I know you, have we met?" She spoke softly. "How do you know who my parents are?" "My, my, you waste no time, you are as inquisitive as you are beautiful. To answer your first question, no my sweet, we have not been properly introduced, shall I do that now? I am Menkaraa Setetsenra, son of the King Menkaure Sebekra Setetsenra III. Yes, we have met but you were in quite a bit of a rush, and we saw only glimpses of each other." Sarset replied, "Will you remain in the shadows or will I see your face?" "I am content to look at you from the shadows for now my love. I would not want to press your fragile senses at this time, seeing how you are trying to recover from an unusual couple of days." Sarset interrupted, "I am at a disadvantage sir, you seem to know quite a bit about my doings and I know only your name, Menkaraa did you say?"

27

She wondered how this man, if he was a man, hiding in the shadows knew her name and so much about her. Reading her mind, Menkaraa stepped into the candlelight of the room, she gasped, "It is you, the man in the woods, why have you brought me here, what do you want from me?" "Calm my dear; I simply kept the woods from swallowing you. I mean you no harm. Have you not bathed, have you not eaten, and have you not found rest? I extend my hospitality to you and I ask that you simply talk with me."

His eyes pierced through her. Menkaraa could tell that his royalness weakened her. Sarset searched his form; he was truly a beautiful man. He stood six feet two inches tall, the image of an African prince of royal blood, strong cheekbones, chiseled jaw line, full lips. His goatee perfectly trimmed, and those striking locks flowing down to his shoulders like branches on the tallest tree. The pupils of his eyes were a light brown, unusual, but his eyeball was white with a tinge of red that seemed to not always be present. His body was sculpted like a god, shoulders broad and round, arms long, ripped, and sinewy. On his bulging biceps, he wore carved gold two-inch clamps, and about his neck hung a gold amulet of an ancient god or symbol. Sarset was arrested by his imposing physical presence, but she felt her edginess ease a bit.

Menkaraa's sudden exposure of his form had brought Sarset to her feet with questions, she managed to sit back in her chair. "Forgive me sir, I meant no disrespect, It's just that what I saw in the woods the other night, and my concern for my elderly parents has caused me to forget my place." Menkaraa was amused by her humbleness, "you have no place young one, and in my abode, you are an honored guest and loved being." She watched him walk almost glide to the matching chair that sat in front of her. She looked into his face and asked soberly, "Menkaraa who are you? Who are your people? Where do you come from? And what do you want from me?" "I will answer all your questions my dear, but when I begin the tale I have only one request of you." Sarset replied, "and what is that sir?" "That you listen intently and reserve judgment for a night's rest." She stood, walked around to the back of her chair as if she would hear no tale, her back was to him and his presence behind her was cold, like an opening door on an early winter morning. She shivered and stepped around back to her seat. "Okay, let's hear your tale" she said as she occupied her seat and tentatively placed her eyes on him and waited for the words. He too stood at first, as if he was going to renege on his words, stepping with his back to her. He smiled to himself and gently seated himself in the chair that was facing her without taking what looked like a step. He saw by her eyes she was surprised at his speed but also fascinated. Menkaraa pondered where to start, the beginning? The middle? The now? His words came from a far away place, slow at first, measured, "I

will tell you of a time before your people, before your people's people,

and when the earth as you know it was young and full of promise."

CHAPTER FIVE

I will begin by telling you about my lineage and beloved homeland. Into this scenario was born my father King Menkaure Sebekra Setetsenra III, King of Kemet, Lord of blood, Warrior King, and God among Men. Lord Sebekra was heir to the throne of Kemet, what the common refer to as Egypt, a foul name to my ancestors that lived and developed that once great land. My father told me he was born in 5200 b.c.e. (before the common era), his father and mother and their father and mother lived in the great southern city of Abu, which translated means elephant. My family, the Setetsenra clan, was known as the great elephant dynasty. We were the architects of many of the early ideas of building temples, and monuments to our motifs of gods and goddesses and our kings and queens. These early structures in Abu spread throughout the eastern part of Akebulan (ancient name of Africa). Our city was a wonder in this southern region of Kemet.

Let me try to describe to you its beauty. It sat on the banks of the Great River Aur (what you know as the Nile), whose beginning flow was unknown and believed to be flowing from the very throne of the God Ptah, his name means "He whom created the first of our Kings." The land was fertile and every green thing that grew on the earth was present. The sweetest fruit trees to the healthiest agriculture, plants, beans, vegetables, melons and greens. The Aur River rushed past our banks bringing the fresh mountain water and dark soil to our animals and crops. We possessed plenty, and famished for nothing. Ours was a haven of peace and development, a civilization that still surpasses modern ones. The God King, Menkaure, my grandfather, he who was the personification of God to us, supervised our country. The people were treated fairly and shared in the administration of daily activities, they brought before the King and his entourage of wise men and priest and scribes, the affairs of the land.

My grandfather had commissioned the development of the land that our armies had secured in the north. We did not have to shed much blood because the people of this region recognized the Royal Family of Abu as a Great House. The only reason for military presence was to keep the unwanted enemies of Kemet off the holy land that was all of Kemet.

My father ascended the throne as all of his people before him. At the passing of the 'Great Elephant', the whole of the country mourned from Abu all the way to Waset the far northern city called The Scepter where I was born, when they learned about my grandfather's death. I never quite recovered, so I became studious and meditative. My eight brothers, of whom I was the ninth son, were busy in the affairs of my father's new kingdom. From my oldest brother Rahotep, who looked upon us as his little brothers, to my brother just before me Menmare Seti, who despised being treated as a younger sibling. Our household was a home of business and royalty.

When my mother, the beautiful Nefertari, assembled us to eat, it was pageantry. The great doors in our palace that open to the dining area were breathtaking. The large handcrafted circular table that my brother Khufu designed and built was covered with every manner of good food and drink. The walls were adorned with paintings of the men and women of my family. At either side of the north end of the room were two statuettes of my father - wondrous pieces. The craftsmen captured the regality of my father. Even though it stood imposing over the room, my father dressed in war crown, and his battle armor was astounding.

We would stand at our places until my eldest brother entered and my father and mother would follow. My father as an imposing king, every bit six feet one inch tall, strong build, short tight locks, which grew longer as he became older. He showed just a little hint of gray in his hair, being the father of nine sons appeared to mark his hair slightly. My mother beside him, appearing as tall because of the crowns she wore, was the most beautiful woman I had ever seen. A face like a diamond, high cheekbones, soft dark cat like eyes. Skin as smooth and rich as the sweetest cream on our dining table. I loved her, she would move in the night as the servants prepared me for sleep. And would appear at my sleep chamber each night and say, "Good night sweet prince, one day, you too shall rule a kingdom."

I sought her in the day as a child to ask her all the questions I stored in my mind. "Why mother has grandfather left us to go rule in the underworld?" She would place her soft hands on my face and say, "Why, little prince, it is the fate of all great kings of Kemet, to leave this earth plane and rule in another dimension. If his majesty Menkaure had stayed in this dimension, your father would never have become King." I of course knew her answers; I just loved to hear her say them to me.

Menkaraa caught himself, and apologized to Sarset, "I digressed, let me get to the essence of the tale." Sarset simply smiled. "My lord, take your time, I have nowhere to go." "Well," he said, as his voice took on that tone of far away. We would sit as a family after the chant in unison "All hail the regent of Kemet, sovereign of the land, harbinger of hotep, (peace) keeper of the gates of the North and South, East and West. Hail the mother of the two lands, nurturer of babes, educator of the scribes, vein of the nation." The servants would leave and we would feast on the meal set before us. No one, apart from us, was allowed to see the king eat. I wondered as a child why that was so, and remembered to file that away as a question to ask my mother when I went looking for her later.

My brother Rahotep would be the first to break the silence at the meal table. He might ask my brother Khufu how construction was going in the kingdom. He generally began, "Well my lord, the temple in Itet Tani is fairing well, the inscribers and painters are arguing over scheduling time, but the work will be completed soon." To which my brother's Sesostris or Rameses would say, "Do you need a regiment of soldiers to arbitrate their dispute?" Khufu would quickly respond, "No thank you brother, the scribes and painters are simple men not warriors." Rameses would simply grunt "humph," to that response, and begin a dissertation on the art of war. I was simply fascinated at the exchanges of my family. Father and mother would just observe and speak only if the young men at the table became heated at each other. When my father spoke "enough," everyone became silent, he was convincing like that.

The people of Waset loved my father and mother and revered them as children loved and respect their parents. They helped build many of the state projects, providing manual labor and artistic expertise. This afforded the people work in their slow season of work, and it gave my father great allegiance from them. The only absolute control my father did not have over the land was the priest. They were a wayfaring lot, never staying in one region of the kingdom for long periods. Creating various gods and goddesses for the people to pay homage to. The sect that worshipped my family was large and odious. Led by the nefarious Apep, an old cruel priest that taught spells and magic to his neophytes. He lavished himself in the wealth of the kingdom and presided over every spiritual exercise in the land. There were no new deities accepted, unless he cleared it first. No new temples were built unless the deities had spoken to him that it was okay.

The tale that gave him his cruel authority was that he could conjure up evil upon his foes, and had done so for my grandfather. My father was not disturbed by his fabled power but did keep him close to watch his movements. My brother Sanakht, whose duty was to keep the sacred crypts of our ancestors, once said that Apep spoke harshly at him over a concern about grave robbers. It was not a significant thing, but he recalled it just the same because of the exchange of the evil one. He said when the conversation became heated he shouted at Apep, "who do you think rules Kemet, my father Menkaure or Apep?" He said he swore he heard the evil thing turn away and utter quietly, "Menkaure for now."

I remember my father's reaction; he placed his gold ladle spoon down very gently and looked to Sanakht, "You did not ask him to clarify his meaning Sanakht?" My brother answered father as if he caught him by surprise. "Sire I was not sure if he said the words or if I was hearing the winds echoing in the crypts." "Then you should not repeat such reprehensible words." My father stood from his seat somewhat agitated. Ahmose my brother, who was the keeper of the libraries interjected, "Father, it is most probable that Apep spoke the words and means you harm. You know historically the priest of Kemet are a fickle lot, they worship all manner of different movements and events on the planet." My father turned his head in the direction of Ahmose and said, "Do you suggest fickleness would cause a man to hate God?" "I simply offer the possibility of the statement having been spoken father," Ahmose meekly stated.

My father was disturbed now, and he stood further from his place turned his back to us all and spoke with a forceful tone. "I will not be controlled by the priest or any other superstitious clan. If such words have been spoken against God, I expect the men in this house to bring me the evidence, and not prattling tales, or whisperings of chamber crypts." He turned back to us and looked cautiously at each person sitting at the table. "An old wise man like Apep is to be watched, my father, told me to keep him close so as to hear his voice, and he said, if I ever hear his voice getting louder than my own." I waited to hear my father finish, but the words did not come. He just smiled and said, "Enough of this clamorous talk, let's finish our meal and speak of the good in Waset," and with that, he sat back at his place and finished his dinner.

"I did not know then but that was the beginning of the woes for Kemet. You see Sarset, as I learned later Apep at that very moment was casting incantations and summoning an evil never seen in Waset before."

In the temple of Wadi Maharaka, Apep was in the inner most sanctuary of the sacred chamber; here only the clean and holy were permitted. Apep in the center of the room was casting a most unclean tirade. "Oh dark gods of night, drinker of blood, deliver your servant the throne of Kemet." The torchlight cast an ominous shadow on the temple walls, the chanting and flickering of the light unsettling for those who fear such things. Apep repeated this calling, like a wailing animal, flailing his hands and throwing himself upon the ground. Where there was only one shadow writhing about on the wall like a helpless rag toy, suddenly there appeared another, faint at first, but growing at each passing second of the mad priest's words.

Apep felt the room grow chill, his breathe showed small vapors of condensation as if he was standing on the Snowcap Mountains of Kilimanjaro. The torches went out one by one until there was only one left flickering in the room. A voice jumped out of the darkness. "You are quite animated priest," the voice in the chamber clattered. Apep looked to the darkest corner of the once well-lit room. "Who speaks?" The figure did not completely reveal himself to the mad priest, he seemed to stretch his neck out of the dark shadow and reveal only his head in the faint light. He resembled the foreigners of the northlands who we called the people of the caves. The legends spoke of pale skin people who crawled on all fours and painted themselves blue, ate raw flesh and drank blood of animals and each other. His hair was long and stringy like pieces of straw attached indiscriminately on his head. His face was long and unshaven, his brow protruded over his eyes and they were fire red like the reddest ruby. "Have you forgotten your chant already little man, or were you just being witty." His lips spread as if laughing revealing a mouth full of tarnished teeth, four of which were very pronounced; sharp like that of a large jungle cat.

Apep apparently recovered from the suddenness of his appearance. "Well what are you called pale demon." He muttered. He drew his head back into the shadows and stepped out into the light of the single torch. "You little blackamoor, can call me prince of the undead. I just happen to be hunting in this area, and heard your little ditty; did you really imagine a drinker of blood would respond to such childish prattle?' "Childish prattle," Apep was offended as the words leapt out of his throat, "I am the high priest of all of Kemet, second only to the king. You will keep that irreverent tongue of yours still and do my bidding." The laugh came slow at first like an irritable discomfort in the stomach, and then it accelerated into an uncontrollable delirium. As the foreigner regained his decorum, he spoke in a cheeky tone. "Your bidding, he repeated again as if he was stunned, your bidding! No my misguided fool," and as quick as you could follow, he seized Apep by his throat and lifted the priest off his feet.

Apep struggled trying to pry the hands of the demon from his gagging breath. "I am the king here and you are the servant, now that, that is clear, take me to this so called king of yours." Apep fell to the ground like a great stone, gasping for precious air that his lungs had been deprived of by the demon. He struggled to his feet and exclaimed that it was not possible for him to take him to the king. "The royal guards would cut us down immediately at the sight of you." "I care not about this useless land or the guards you have to protect it. I will see this god king your people have created, and I will judge if he is a god or just another ambitious man. I have a thing for ambitiousness."

His eyebrows were raised in excitement at the thought. Apep was stunned; he began to realize this creature meant to do something other than give him the throne of Kemet. He stammered, "And if you judge our King to be ambitious, then what?" The vampire did not answer directly; he snatched Apep by the back collar of his tunic and levitated out of the causeway of the temple and skyward saying only. "We shall see, we shall see." Apep flailed in the air as he lost his grounding on the stone floor."

My father was a very ritualistic king. He had tended the last details of the day and was practicing his great swordsmanship. Into the open sill of the practice chamber came Apep like a tossed bundle of clothing. His body hit the floor with a thud and my father was startled at the anguished sound of his painful cry from such ill treatment. Menkaure watched as the priest tried to gather himself and stand. He had never seen the priest so disheveled and a skewed, it was somewhat amusing at first but when my father looked to where the body came, and saw a figure never seen in his kingdom, he gripped his sword tighter in his hand.

"What evil have you brought to the house of Setetsenra," he charged the priest. The priest mumbled unintelligible words at my father and fell back on his knees in reverence. The stranger stood in the windowsill watching the groveling of the foolish man. He gently began to rise from the window without the use of his hands; he had them crossed in front of his chest. His body just moved upward from the stone like some flying bird. My father drew his sword up as if to ready for some attack. He was not impressed with the feat of the man; he thought it some trick like the magician in Kemet. He commanded Apep to explain. "What is this pale magician doing in my house?"

The stranger descended toward my father, he spoke and said. "Speak not to your worm of a servant direct your words to me." My father responded, "Who are you that the king of Kemet would even acknowledge you." As his feet touched the floor, he looked at my father and then at Apep groveling on the ground and back to my father. "Who I am is of no concern to you, what I am should be your question." He smiled snidely. My father did not respond to his verbal sparring. He simply turned away and made his way to the door to have the guards remove the foul being. "I would not do that if I were you, I came to speak to you, if you call your guards I'll have to rip your throat out and we wouldn't want that now would we."

Suddenly the thing was standing in front of my father, his eyes glowing red now and sinister. He stepped toward my father; my father stepped back, sword drawn once again to ready. "This lump of flesh crying on the floor at your feet, he called out to me god king. It appears he wants this little kingdom delivered to him, imagine that." He moved so swiftly that before my father could raise his sword in his defense, he had gripped the king's wrist and placed his other hand around his throat. His warm foul breath blew at his nostrils, the King's sword dropped from his grasp and rattled to the floor. "Let go of me you foul beast or I assure you, you will live to regret it." The King's words gagged out of his mouth. The foreigner laughed loudly and arrogantly, "Live, did you say live little king? I have not lived in a thousand years, and in that many years I have not seen a god or king that could govern me or speak to me so. You black skins think you are Gods, what do you know of God?" He continued to squeeze my father as he interrogated him. "Has he spoken to you? Does he answer you when you call? Where is this God at this moment when I'm holding his King's life in my very hand?" He laughed even more hysterically. "Oh yeah, you are the god of this land, right?" He tossed my father across the room like so many unwanted things. My father struggled to regain his feet, he coughed and gasped for air as the strangle hold was released. "What do you want?" he managed to eject from his throat. "Ahh, the god speaks to us now. Has a little toss across the room made us equals?"

Menkaure stood now, regained the composure of a royal King of Kemet, and spoke to the thing that just handled him like a ruffian. "I know not who you are foul thing, but I have seen your kind making incursions into our holy land, you are vagabonds and unclean. You appear to have worked some magic to give yourself this advantage over my superior skill and intellect." "Yes little king I am a vagabond, and there are those who call me unclean. As for magic, I reserve that for the superstitious lot like your sniveling priest here. I came here today because I was awe struck at the little kingdom you have built; your temples and stone carvings are like nothing on this earth I have seen. I was just passing through until the mindless beseeching of your priest reached my ear. I just had to see who could be lamenting so loud as to draw an audience to them. After I listen in the dark for a moment, being amused I stepped out of the shadows to speak to him. He was as arrogant as you. So I had to see this god-king face to face to see if he was truly a god or just another tyrant in men's clothing."

The demon seemed to not know what to say next, he wiped the creases from his wrinkled sleeves from tussling with Menkaure. "I must say you have disappointed me so far so I'll offer you this; Menkaure is it? I offer you one chance to save your life." Menkaure took a very ancient fighting stance; very subtle you wouldn't be able to detect he was prepared for an assault. "I will not be bargained with, if you mean me evil then creature it is your move." My father said defiantly. This enraged the visitor he spun toward my father and not anticipating my father's readiness was caught flush in the chest with a sidekick, which drove him across the room on his back and against the wall. My father scurried to his lain sword while the creature tried to regain his footing. As he came up with the sword to render the beast, he was too late; the foreigner was on him wrenching the sword from my father's grasp. He lifted my father by the throat again, "persistent little meal you are," he said condemningly to Menkaure. "What shall I do with you"? In addition, as if a great idea came to him he said, "I will give you this kiss of mine and if you are anything like the god your people think you are, you should survive, if not, you will die in a matter of days." He drew my father's neck to his mouth the impact of his incisor teeth sunk into Menkaure's throat. My father screamed out and struggled, but the transferring of his blood to the creature's mouth was lapsing him into unconsciousness. He could hear the faint sucking sound of this thing on his neck and he thought he could hear him cry out in pain, or satisfaction, he no longer could tell. It appeared the fate of our king was sealed, but suddenly the arm that held my father fell away from the body of the vampire. He roared in agony as my father's body and the things' arm dropped to the floor. The thing turned to see who had struck him so, and there stood the cursed Apep; his blood-filled mouth spewing words at him. "Fool you raise your treacherous hands to me, you sought someone like me with your incantations and pleadings." Apep tried to strike at him again. The vampire simply sidestepped the blow and took the sword from his feeble hands. All he managed to do was give the creature the means to destroy him. With several vicious blows, he struck Apep asunder.

The footsteps of the royal guards could be heard approaching the chamber. The demon dropped the blood soaked blade on the remains of the wicked priest and turned to the arm that was struck off. He picked it up and looked to my father sprawled on the floor like a feeble man, blood from his neck wound opened, and fresh. The sounds of the guards were close; the intruder needed to make his way out. He whispered into my father's unconscious ear, "I have left you a gift blackamoor, use it well or die from it, neither matters to me. We may meet again until then suffer long." His sardonic laugh was heard in the chamber like a jarring noise as he jumped through the window and disappeared.

Menkaraa looked at Sarset she seemed transfixed, "Are you alright my dear?" Sarset nodded; her head was spinning; his tale had snatched her into a world she did not know or understand. A world of kings, queens, blood sucking monsters, and evil priests. What was Menkaraa trying to say to her? Was he mad or was this a true tale that had taken place in some forgotten time? She tried to cloak her shock and amazement. "Forgive me Menkaraa, but such a tale I've never heard before." "It is quite a bit for mortal minds" he responded. Menkaraa stood to offer her some wine to ease her racing heart that he could feel surging. Her thoughts were racing at his vampire mind.

Sarset was not aware that her thoughts were so opened to his perusal. She thought how could this tale take place, when he appeared to be only in his early thirties. "Thirty five to be exact", he interjected. This startled her and she asked how did he answer a question she had not spoken?" I can hear the thoughts of mortals if I concentrate and sift out all the other voices and sounds in this realm." Sarset looked surprised, "I have a simple request, it appears as if we are unequal in many ways; you, reading my thoughts is not fair my lord nor polite". Menkaraa said, "Forgive me lady, I shall not intrude again." He handed her the glass of wine and sat back across from her searching eyes. She sipped at the wine with her soft lips. He could see the question forming in her mind. "What happened to your father and the kingdom of Abu?" "Ah, the tale I shall continue then."

CHAPTER SIX

My father awoke to a throbbing pain in his neck, as his eyes opened, he saw the Priest of Ra around his bedchamber. He could smell incense and the weeping of women servants and the faithful constant praying. Trying to raise himself upon one elbow, he was greeted with a concerned voice, "Do not try to raise my Lord, you have been wounded."

My father slipped in and out of consciousness for days. His life signs became weaker and weaker. "I've left you a gift my little king," the face of the northlander laughed in my father's face. "No, no" Menkaure bolted upright in the bed, eyes blank, sweat pouring down his face. The attendants restrained him, and looked at each other, small incisor teeth crept down onto his lips. What was happening to their king, their eyes asked each other.

The kingdom was experiencing unrest after the word had spread of an attempt on the king's life. The people wanted to see the God King, and to be assured that their beloved leader was well. Bak, my father's most trusted vizier met with the elders of the family; my mother, Rahotep, Khufu, Sanakht, Userkaf, and Ahmose. The Great Queen Nefertari spoke first, and asked Bak how her beloved fared. Bak, a loyal servant of our people and friend of my father, voice stumbled at first and then he spoke. "Our sire is resting and being watched and attended to around the setting and rising of the sun. I think we should speak to the people, a few days have passed and they have not seen the face of their ruler, since the word has spread that he is ill." Rahotep the eldest of my brothers said, "How grave is the attack on my father?" Bak turned to him and said, "We are not certain yet, but the King is strong and showing signs of coming to."

Userkaf, the oldest of my warrior brothers, slammed his palm on the table where they all sat and yelled out. "Apep and his clan of evil shall be dealt with, let's talk of that matter. We cannot let the people see us be weak or hesitant to the priest clans." "Oh of course, let's start a civil war among the people, so you and Sesostris and Rameses can roar your chariots and swords through the land." My brother Ahmose said sardonically. As Userkaf was about to respond, Rahotep intercepted the volley of words that would have been exchanged between my brothers. "Brothers, mother and lord Bak, we must act as if Menkaure was still making the decisions here and not ill. Now first we must be sure that the enemy that has hurt our Lord is either caught or dead. Then we must deal with whoever got him so close to the king in the first place. If that means dealing with the Apep clan, then we must be wise and careful." Bak agreed with the words of Rahotep, as did my mother, Ahmose and Khufu. Userkaf agreed only out of respect for my mother and Bak. They agreed to schedule a city meeting so that the citizens could know what was happening in the kingdom.

As they made their way out of the hall, Userkaf approached Rahotep. "You are the oldest of us Ra, and I will say this only once more, if Khufu and Ahmose insult the generals of the imperial army any more." Rahotep cut him off, "Userkaf, stop this inane bickering among intellect and soldiers. We need both as much as they need the other. I will not referee over this persistent dislike you all have for each other. Kemet is in dire need of cool heads and well-planned ideas, not squabbling brothers." The weight of his oldest brother's reprimand struck him full force and Userkaf yielded. "As you speak sire, heir to the throne of Kemet, I bid you peace." Rahotep watched as his brother walked away. He understood he had to be clear and focused because his brothers were all men of action and he needed them as much as Kemet did.

At the gates of Waset, the people were stirring, trickles at first, then a few more, and then a swelling crowd. From my father's window, the attendants were distracted by the commotion of the citizens. As they turned back to the king's bed, suddenly the door swung open, "My Lord", Bak spoke as he beheld the King sitting erect as if he had only been sleeping and was now ready to arise. My mother and Rahotep who had caught up with them stepped into the room. Nefertari surprised at the sight of Menkaure sitting up and conscious ran to embrace him. She fell on his neck and sobbed, "My love, are you all right? I worried for your life." Rahotep looked sharply to the servants. "Avert your eyes and leave the presence of God and Goddess Setetsenra, speak not from your lips anything that you have beheld with your eyes." The servants frightened by Rahotep's stern words, fell to their knees and wailed together, "As thou has spoke sire, we live only to obey the voice of God." They scurried from the room. All eyes were now on Menkaure, he lifted my mother's head from his shoulders and asked her, "Why are you so shaken and what is the noise I hear at the gate of our home?" He stood and walked to the window. "Why are the people of Waset gathering at the gate?" Bak stepped toward my father with his head bowed. "My Lord they have heard of you falling ill, and gather only to see you." "Father", Rahotep interjected, "Do you remember anything that has happened to you?" Menkaure turned back to the people standing in the room, his eyes looked to Rahotep his eldest son, looking every bit ready to ascend the throne of Kemet, then to Bak his most humble and loyal vizier, ever vigil and waiting. When his eyes reached Nefertari, the beautiful one, which is the literal translation of my mother's name, he spoke. "Call the attendants back, have them bathe and dress me I will speak to the people and ease their minds." Mother stood and walked over to my father, kissed him on his cheek and bade him hotep (peace). Rahotep bowed to father and said, "As you speak father so be it." Turning, he closed to doors behind him.

Bak, my father's friend, stepped into the background of the room, as the attendants appeared and began to wash and clothe the king; he wondered why he showed no signs of the trauma inflicted upon him. The bite marks they found on his neck after washing his throat area had closed and appeared completely vanished. Except for the red tinge in his otherwise clear eyes, he seemed well.

His mind slipped back to the days that led to now. Bak heard the sound of strange laughter not like someone amused though, different. As he quickly approached the practice room, the doors were wide open and the royal guards were filling the entrance. They stepped aside at his appearance, just beyond the shoulders of the regal guards of Kemet, was a sight he had not witnessed before two guards were trying to associate the pieces of flesh and blood dismembered on the floor. Bak gasped "No, is it our lord." The guards pointed across the room, his fears were somewhat alleviated. There, the men were trying to stop the blood flow from Menkaure's neck wound that looked life threatening.

Bak commanded the guards at the door to retrieve Rahotep the King's eldest.

"What did you see when you entered the room?" Bak asked anxiously. The blood was pooling at the body of Menkaure, and the pressure did not seem to be abating it. "We heard a commotion, thinking the King was only sparring, then the cry of Apep the priest was heard and we began to approach the door. When we opened it we heard the laughter of someone or something that appeared to be going through that window." Bak said, "We are thirty to forty feet up, how?" "We looked to the window and saw only a strange shadow." Rahotep interrupted the conversation, "What has happened to the Regent of Kemet?" His answer came swiftly to him, as he saw his father's body lying in a coagulated mat of blood. "Lift him; bring him to the royal chamber." Bak spoke, "Is that wise my lord." "Will we let him die here on the floor of this chamber?" Rahotep shot back.

The soldiers lifted the King and bore him to the room. Bak ordered the guards to search the city for a possible suspect. "Search every hovel and Nome, leave no place uninvestigated." "Bak" my father's voice brought Bak back to the present. "Assemble the court and let's stop this rumbling at the gates of our beautiful city." Bak cleared his perplexed eyes and turning toward the door hesitated, turning back to Menkaure, he asked.

"Sire, may I speak alone to you for a moment before you speak to the people?" Menkaure motioned the servants out. Bak carefully approached his master. "My Lord, what do you remember?" Menkaure looked at his friend puzzlingly and said, "Apep the evil one tried to slay God and failed," as he searched Bak's eyes for a challenge. "I cannot tell the people that a northlander laid his corruptible hands on my personage." Menkaure reluctantly let out. "Bak, I don't remember everything but such a tales as I have seen would terrify the people." "As you live my Lord, I serve you. I meant not to question your authority or rule."

The guards told me that they saw a strange shadow; I pulled him to the side as they took you from the room. He said the shadow was pale like the moon itself and it appeared to have an arm in its hand." "Let's continue this later most honored adviser"; my father clasped the arm of Bak. "We must not keep the people any longer." The coldness of my father's skin when he touched him startled Bak but he smiled approvingly back and bowed his head. As my father's entourage led him to the great Hypostyle Hall of Judgment, Bak whispered a prayer to the ancients that Menkaure his beloved King would not be found lacking this night.

CHAPTER SEVEN

The great Edifice was a wonder on earth, nowhere on the continent or of this time was a building so imposing and beautiful. Its tall pillars exploded into lotus flowers at the height of the ceiling. The murals of battles, my fathers' forbearers had engaged and won painted in rich colors of blue and red and green, so lovely as to distract one from the proceedings in the chamber. The skill and art work unseen in our new world, and when you walked between the path of God; statues of the twenty five successive kings, names not uttered from the lips of foreigners or enemies your breath was taken. These limestone forms carved in the quarries of ancient Kemet stood imposing along the walk to the throne seat. Your sandal clacking along the carefully smooth stone floor, its echo returning to you two, three fold. As these men frozen in the time of their glory listened to each small step you took.

My father took his place on the seat of gold, which was carved in the shape of a huge smooth U with curling outward arms; he rested his arms on the throne chair. Menkaure looked out from the seat in front of him, closes to him on his left was the great wife and goddess of Kemet Nefertari, to her left the sires of Kemet my brothers and I. He looked to the right his most personal royal guards, and to their right, the advisors of the court, except Bak the chief vizier stood to my father's right shoulder.

The people were allowed in now that all were present. As they gathered to the front of the edge of my father's entourage, the guards stepped forward to buffer the pressing crowd. Menkaure began to speak, "People of Kemet children of Ra, there is much I must tell you, and much you want to know or have already surmised. First I am well as you can see." The people murmured in unison "Yes, yes." The advisors raised their hands for the people to be still. My father continued, "The old priest Apep is dead, a victim of his own demise. The news caused a flurry of questions amongst the people in attendance, none of which the King sought to acknowledge or answer. The Royal Guards admonished the crowd to return to silence, and they quickly responded.

Upon returning the people to silence, the sound of protest came from the back in the assemblage. "How does a man cut asunder himself?" The crowd stirred and began chattering and repeating the question to one another. An old man, who seemed to gain the respect of the crowd, paraphrased the question, "Yes, how did Apep meet his end?" Menkaure was not bothered by the crowd's insistence on the question being answered. He was however bothered by the tone of the original questioner. He commanded that Userkaf have the guards bring the questioner forward to stand before Ra (sun) and question him face to face. The guards quickly snatched the man and brought him forward. The people parted and gave up the man in the back who had asked the question.

A familiar face, Asret, the acting priest of the Apep clan, now stood exposed to the throne. His head was clean-shaven as is the custom of learning priest and neophytes. His clothing somewhat ruffled by the thronging crowd and handling of the guards were finely made. He bowed his head and said nothing. Rameses my brother asked, "have the crocodiles swallowed your tongue now that you stand before God?" Asret still did not raise his head to my father or answer Rameses.

My father stood, "Asret will you tell this assemblage how Apep came to his end since you are not pleased with my rendition." "Sss-sire he began stumbling, I meant no disrespect. It's just that the imperial armies are rousting us and have not told us why. They threw the remains of our chief priest at the door of our temple. Imagine us opening the cloth to see the rendered body of our leader? "When I asked for an audience with you and was told that, that would not happen." Father looked to Bak and then his sons; none gave him a clue as to the statements being true. He turned from Asret and sat back in his chair. "Asret," my father began, "your scheming leader, and old friend has attempted to dethrone the house of Setetsenra, in his failed attempt he was slain by his comrade." He now lifted his head to the King, "We did not sanction such an act or knew of it my Lord!" "This may be true Asret but the deed has been perpetrated through your sect and I will not tolerate anarchical plots in my kingdom."

The people began to roar, "take the priest, take the priest." My father raised his hand. "People of Waset, be still and don't behave as children." The reprimand had its desired effect as the crowd sound died to silence. "We will give you Asret, as my father looked back to him. Five Ra (sun) days, to leave this kingdom if on the fifth day you or your clan are on Kemet soil whosoever finds you shall slay you or them." He stood and pointed to the scribes, "As I have spoken it, so shall you write it." Asret bolted from his knees where he fell at the pronouncement of the King. "No sire, no this is my home, this is my place of birth, have mercy on me, have pity." My mother in all her beauty stood expressionless. He pleaded with her; she slowly turned her back as did my brothers and the advisors, and finally Bak. My father stood and proclaimed "Asret, the house of Setetsenra has turned its back to you, and I have no succor for you, guards lead him from here."

The people were stunned and simply watched as the royal guards led Asret from the hall, his begging and pleading falling upon the stone ears of my father and the statues that lined the hall. Menkaure stood and spoke to the loyal people assembled, "Go back to your homes, and let those who could not enter this hall this day know that their God and their King is well. Let not priest or kin persuade you otherwise. I stand and will find the accomplices of Apep and I will bring a swift end to this matter. Go, hotep (peace) to you." The crowd exited the hall chanting "Hotep to Menkaure protector of our land, Sovereign of Waset, God of Upper and Lower Kemet." My father waited until the last person was out of the room, he dismissed his entourage and left with Bak and Nefertari. Bak said, "You spoke wisely tonight my Lord, and your fairness to Asret will be remembered for some time." "Yes my sweet the people see you as a just and righteous leader." Nefertari submitted. My father walking slightly ahead of the two of them said only, "I have made an enemy this night and sleep will come hard to me from this night on."

Suddenly, my father cried out in pain and fell upon the wall. Clutching his stomach, Bak rushed to him and bore his weight upon him. "What is this strange pain in my body that I feel, it is like a hunger denied?" My mother frantically asked, "My love are you alright?" Bak helped my father to his chamber and assured my father it was only a mild hunger pain it would subside after he received some nourishment. My mother agreed and dismissed herself to go have the meal prepared. Bak helped my father ease down into a chair. His love for my father was deep; seeing him in such great pain grieved him.

Menkaure's sweat came in great drops and his body was going limp. Bak checked my father for a pulse and found none, he reeled back in fear, his mind was racing is his king dead, what will he do, how will he explain the suddenness of the King's death. He regained his composure and pressed his head to his sire's chest, he heard no sound not the inhaling of lungs or the flowing of blood to the heart. Bak was defeated, he sank into the lap of his dead king, and his tears came hard and unstoppable. He repeatedly cried, "No, no, no." As he was bowed at the feet of Menkaure, he slowly gathered himself up. He looked at the king, for what was the last time in his mind and heart. "I bid you hotep, most benevolent one." He turned and reached for the door, hesitating with his hands on the door handle, Bak felt a chill on the back of his neck, the kind you feel when you think you are alone and then suddenly something or someone seems to be in the room with you. Fear is a strange emotion. It overtakes you before you have time to brace and react with courage. He spun around and was so startled by what he saw, he repelled upon the crease of the doors. Standing before him was a man he once thought he knew but somehow had transformed or rose from the dead.

Dreads hanging like a curtain over his face, Menkaure stood before Bak. Where he was moments ago still and lifeless, he now slowly raised his head revealing eyes that were completely black. There was no white, or red or pupil, totally blank and dark. His teeth were as white as fine cultured pearls, the incisor teeth pressing on his lower lip. My father spoke deep and quiet, almost like a whisper. "Bak my loyal one, what is wrong, why so uneasy?" Now, frozen before his king, unnerved at the sudden appearance of him at his back. The words stammered out of his mouth, "Not...nothing...my Lord." My father could hear the sound of his servant's blood racing in his heart, he smelled the sweat creeping upon his brow and pooling to the surface of his pores in his skin. Menkaure's eyes darted all over his servant like a hunting animal. "Bak tell me, no more riddles, and no more about hunger unquenched what has happened to me? I see and hear on a new level, I sense the fluid in your heart, its path and course. I feel your terror, your fear."

Bak stepped to the side of my father's pressing questions; Menkaure's dark eyes followed his movement. As he moved past my father, trying not to appear frightened, he said. "My Lord I tried to do the best for you that I could. When the royal guard arrived we tried to stop the bleeding, you slipped into a coma. In two days your skin went cold and the physicians could not find a pulse or heart beat." Menkaure with his back to his servant spoke without turning to him. "Yet I stand before you Bak, walking speaking, account for this." The tone in my father's voice was distant and cold. "Sire, we feared the rumbling of the people, as regent I assembled your eldest son and beautiful queen, the minister of war Userkaf, your son and wise Ahmose keeper of the books. We agreed that, Rahotep should speak to the crowd with the great Nefertari by his side and quell the stirring of their voices. We stopped only to check in on your condition to find you awake and stirring."

The sound of clapping hands aborted any more exchange between Bak and my father, they both swung to the direction of the off cadence sound. "Bravo, bravo the Blackamoor has survived the kiss, you are stronger than I assumed." Sitting in the chair in the corner of my father's bedchambers sat the accursed foreigner. He sat as if invited in by the King himself. One leg slung over the arm of the chair, enjoying the dissertation of Bak.

Bak was the first to speak at the sight of him. "So, are you the thief at night that would scheme with the enemies of God and bring evil to our most sacred house?" The fiend just grinned at Bak. "You blacks have great descriptive words for me", he laughed amused at himself, "And I give you that. I have no accomplices, as you found when you entered the chamber and saw your king and his most foolish priest sprawled on the floor." Menkaure now interjected, "Creature, what have you done to me and why is this hunger stirring in my stomach that is unlike normal hunger?" "I told you most foolish man", he shot back at my father, "that you should have been more interested in what I was instead of who I was?" He wagged his index finger back and forth like a pendulum clock as if he was scolding a child.

"Sire should I call the royal guards?" Bak asked. "Yes, yes," the stranger entreated, "call the useless men you surround yourself with I will rend them like the chaff in the field, don't you know who and what I am by now fool?" He stood and Bak noticed he had both arms intact. "Have you not asked how I come in and out of your realm at will? You didn't even hear me sitting in this room, while your flatulent words about your ordeal to your pitiful king eased from your mouth and bored me. I am the God in this room" he angrily condemned Bak, "Not this propped up man king here," the thing pointed to my father as he continued, "he doesn't even know that the blood that is racing through his body is no longer the blood of his precious forefathers, but the blood of a much more ancient line then his own."

Menkaure enraged at the accusation said, "and what line is more ancient than the Setetsenra clan monster? You are an aberration in this land, with your pale skin and stringy hair, your eyes, the color of buried stones." This stranger standing before my father, laughed as if all of this

63

was just some joke only he was privy to. "King of Kemet, you are the aberration now; we are brothers of the same blood covenant now. You govern over this land as a God, well now you truly are a God. Though you many never see the sun that you so, worship, ever again, you are now truly eternal, no enemy can stand before you and men are now your servants and meal." How ironic huh?" "What madness is this you are saying," my father stumbled. Blood covenant, men are my meal." The evil one only illustrated to my father what he meant, he pounced on Bak and sunk his teeth into his neck, poor Bak did no even have a chance to scream out. My father wrenched him from his grasp and at the same time saying, "Unhand him fiend." The blood running down the sides of his mouth, crimson on his teeth, his indifferent reply, "As you wish", wiping Bak's blood from the corner of his mouth continued, "but if you don't feed soon this will be an experiment in futility."

My father looked at the wound on his friend's neck and the pain in his stomach and mouth ached at him. He looked at the fiend, he began to understand, "Yes my black King you are me and I am you, a bloodsucker, a vampire." The words screamed in my father's ear, Vampire, Vampire, he dropped the silent body of Bak onto the marble floor. His eyes were blank, as if he had just stepped into another dimension, no sound came from his lips he just stood stone still, blank, as if his mind had vacated its place.

The vampire walked up to him and looked in his face, surprised at my father's shock and inability to speak. "You'll get over it I assure you," he breathed into the face of my father, "I tell you this before I leave, there is no god of this or any other land that can help you now. You will live an eternity of rising and lowering suns. You will suck the blood of other humans and you will grow to despise them, you will either destroy this kingdom or yourself; neither really matters to creatures such as us." He turned to walk away and stopped as if he forgot something important, "Oh yeah, your servant will die if you do not finish the job. Suck the blood slow, and when you feel his heart about to stop withdraw and wait to see if he will survive. Some can bear the embrace, others hearts just can't take it. Goodbye Menkaure, I don't believe we will see each other again. If so, have more to say, ha ha ha ha ha aha!" His parting laughter filled the room and then he was gone.

The exit of the demon was the awakening of my father. He looked at Bak bleeding on the floor, he repulsed at the thought of defiling his friend and most loyal citizen. He thought there had to be another way to save him, to spare his life. Bak's gurgling sounds were driving him mad; he knelt at his side, holding his friend in his arms. "Sorry old friend, I can't find another solution. I must believe what this cursed thing has told me, I can't let you lie here and die."

Menkaure felt his incisor teeth etch out at the appearance of the neck wound, he pressed his mouth at the wound, and the blood came warm at first, sticky not as he imagined it; a little sweet almost delicious. It was like a deep furlong kiss of a lover that he now was locked in with. Bak's heart; it pulsed normal at first, then came surging as if he was running, he listened for its slowing but the embracing was swooning him, he felt as if he was losing consciousness. He pried himself away and sobbed; my father was overcome with the act. Never had a Setetsenra defiled a friend like he just did. He felt utter despair, why didn't he just let Bak die, and he wait for the coming of the sun. Hours passed and my father did not look to see if Bak was alive or dead.

Menkaraa stopped, the tale had taken every bit of his psychological strength, and the memories of his father tore at the fiber of his sanity. His head dropped and his eyes were not visible to Sarset. She was stunned; looking at Menkaraa's bowed head, she wondered why he had entrusted this tale to her? The quiet of the room was loud, his voice no longer filling the space and unfamiliarity of the surrounding walls. "Menkaraa, are you okay?" She asked cautiously. The stillness of his voice after such a tale coming forth from his mouth was deafening. "If you no longer wish to talk about these things then speak no further." He looked up and seemed to be still lost in the tale. "My dear lady forgive my hesitancy, only when I recount this tale do I realize how much I have really lost. The humanity of my family's life, the majesty, the discipline, the splendor, all gone now, all just a cruel memory of a time and life that mattered."

He stood now and walked over to the window. The darkness did not give him a caress like the many nights that he stared at this woman behind him from the cover of the trees. He didn't want to finish the tale; he didn't want to talk about his family any longer. Night was escaping and dawn was soon to arrive. If creatures like him could look sorrowful, when he turned back to Sarset, she saw a being whose expression was so disheartened; she felt compelled to console him. She walked toward him and touched his hand. Menkaraa's head was lowered. Sarset raised his chin with her forefinger, their eyes locked and she spoke, "you have witnessed much Menkaraa, I thought the pain and loss I have known and experienced was unbearable. I have stayed sane by caring for my mother and my father. You are alone and that has to be the hardest part of your journey." She caressed the side of his face with the palm of her hand, his hard strong face seemed to warm to her touch and the sorrow appeared to be easing and flowing away. He reached for her hand that was on his cheek and pulled it away he softly said to her. "I don't deserve the sympathy or pity from one as beautiful as you. Sarset, I'm a vile creature, an aberration of mankind. I have lost my way these past hundred years. I was once the son of a great ancient king and kingdom, I now run from the enemies of my father and his past. The actions and decisions that he made are visited on me. I have no home, I know no one, I am at the end of this journey, I saw you and for some strange reason, I thought I saw Kemet again. I watched you from the cover of the woods many nights. I left you gold in a precious box when I saw you were close to famished. I listened to your sweet songs as you toiled in your kitchen. These things I did thinking I could touch my humanity again if I touched you."

She digested his words so dismal and gloomy. She stood in front of him looking at his face as he tried to avoid her eyes and asked him what he meant his fathers enemies. "Is someone chasing you Menkaraa, are you in danger?" Drawing a breath of air into his lungs he exhaled. "I remember my father and mother one warm African night. They sat by the pond overlooking the garden. She did not come to me that night and bid me sleep well. I was disturbed by that and went seeking her. I found them at the pond's edge, my mother's feet dangling in the water. I stood in the cover of the gardens brush and watched them. My mother's head rested in his lap and they laughed, talked, and kissed like young lovers. I could not hear the full conversation. What I saw that night I've never told any one. Menkaure began to kiss my mother lovingly about the neck and she swooned as most lovers do. Her feet splashed playfully in the water, and I started back for my room before I intruded on their personal intimacy. Suddenly the sound of my mother's feet in the water sounded different not playful any more but frantic, I turned back to see my father embracing my mother in a kiss I have come to know all too well. I screamed out "no!" My father turned and saw me; suddenly behind me, strong hands gripped my mouth. A familiar voice spoke in my squirming ear, "Be still young whelp, it was not intended for you to see such things right now." I felt my feet leaving contact with the ground as I was lifted and carried back toward the palace.

Sarset was stunned; she stepped back and said, "Why? Why would Menkaure do such a thing to your mother?" She walked back to the chair by the slowly dying fire and sat down. "I felt he had such honor and dignity. You described him as coming from a history of honorable men." Before she could look back where she left Menkaraa standing by the window, he was sitting again in the chair gazing at her. This startled her. "You ask me questions that I have not appeased myself Sarset." "Is this what you have planned for me?" She asked presumably. He was hurt now, and she could see in his eyes that her words had cut him to the quick. "I did not mean that Menkaraa, that was unfair of me. It is just that", she hesitated for the right words to come. "I felt like Menkaure and Nefertari were one of the great love stories that I have always dreamed of. There is so much pain and hate in this land now, with the foreigners defiling the land and the wrenching of families apart through the slave trade. There is very little left of true love and life here." "Who has filled your mind with such whimsical tales of life and true love?" Menkaraa shot back. "Why my mother and father of course," she answered.

"I have seen my father before he became ill and life here in Karnak became unbearable he loved my mother like the sun. My father too came from a line of honorable men. Maybe not as rich and powerful as your father's clan but he has tended this land as a farmer and handler of cattle for decades. When the thieves of the land appeared, my father protected us for as long as he could. He never sold his cattle to them or his produce. My brothers worked the land with my father and they were a formidable team. They worked the land and cattle while the others rotated in and out of positions. Never allowing them to be surprised or taken unawares by cattle thieves or land burners. Through all of this he loved my mother most of all, not the land not the cattle not even us. He lived for my mother's smile when he came in from work. I would watch him gather her up in his arms and say, "Tuya for you this day I have toiled and kept watch." Then lavish her with kisses and hugs. It was this whimsical sight, which filled my head with such things." He answered her with "Yeah, yeah, you have spoken well."

Menkaraa looked to the window; the light was breaking forth under the sill to the floor. "I must leave now my dear, the sun is pressing me, can we continue this in the night?" "What shall I do till then?" Sarset asked. "I feel imprisoned here in this room confined by whatever is outside the door." "Forgive me – allow me to introduce you to my only friend Ku." He went to the door of the room and let the great lion in. Sarset startled, jumped in her chair like she instinctively would run. Menkaraa told the beast to be still. The lion obeyed and laid down on his stomach looking unimpressed at the woman in the chair. "He will not harm you my dear, I sat him at the door more out of protection for you than to imprison you. I will take him to my sleep chamber. You can explore the house, until the night comes again and I come to you. There is a stocked kitchen and a great library; I hope these occupy your time until dusk. Hotep, sweet one." Menkaraa turned to go out the door; he spoke "come Ku," and the animal jumped to his feet and scurried after his falling footsteps. Sarset was exhausted; she slumped in her chair not believing what she had seen and heard thus far.

CHAPTER EIGHT

He climbed down from the covering of the branches of the tree. It was a little difficult for him, but he had managed, he thought, to get the information he was sent for. Bes was a loyal servant; he stood every bit three feet five inches tall. He was a Twi, the foreigners called his people pygmies, he disdained them for it; it was a term of derogatory origin. His ancestors were the seed people of this great continent. Bes's home lies south of this decimated land of Karnak, the great Ituri forest, Home of the Twi, the small peoples of the Olduvai Gorge region. The keepers of this place have allowed after all that his people have taught them, to be subjugated by the children of sand dwellers and northern caves. He, Bes, knew the old ways were better, living next to nature, having only what you needed, and eating only what would be fresh for a day.

The Twi people understood the sheltering of a nation, keeping undesirables out so that the people are free to grow undisturbed for thousands of years. This is how the great monuments were built and started. The Kemetians kept foreigners out long enough to develop and learn science and art and geometry and geophysics, language both written and spoken; and his people were there at the beginning, even when the vampire king dynasty began.

He hurried along the trail in the darkness, knowing very well that many predators in the night could mistake him for a small animal that they could pounce on. He had someone to meet very soon that did not have patience for tardiness. Bes smiled like the jovial carnival performers that came to Karnak every season, his master would be so pleased with this new information on his wayward target. In fact, maybe this time he would really keep his promise and allow him to go back home.

Bes reached the edge of the forest and looked back once more to assure himself of the location he saw the man enter the covering. How vain, he thought or typical of these ancient creatures, his hidden entryway was positioned true to the star of Ausar. He shook his head and headed for the small town.

Sarset was tired; the tale she had just walked through with Menkaraa was incredible. She decided to sleep for a few hours and then rise and take Menkaraa up on his offer to explore her surroundings. Strangely, she believed him when he told her that her parents were being well cared for at home. While she missed them, she knew that she would see them soon enough. The bed was inviting, the soft pillows and silk soft sheets and warm covering engulfed her body and swallowed her into sleep. She mumbled softly and drifted off.

Menkaraa entered his chamber not exhausted in the manner that a human would feel after such a night of events but rather exposed like a secret long kept. He had no idea why he revealed so much of himself to Sarset; her familiarity was almost like the ancients speak of ancestors revisiting you in the vessel of someone or something new. He knew this was a fable or was it. She did resemble his mother so, the great queen of Kemet. He could feel the sun that he missed so desperately, warming the earthen chamber he stood in. What would the night hold for him, how would he ask Sarset to be with him and what would her answer be? He walked to the door and closed it on the side of the lion, which was lying in front of the opening. His feet lifted off of the floor without taking a step, he had levitated and turned around effortlessly and began to be parallel to the floor as if a cushion of air was holding him suspended above it, his body drifted toward the bed. When his form was correlated over the mattress of the huge bed, he slowly descended and before his head touched the pillow, his vampire eyes were closed.

Bes did not like this city; in fact, he didn't like any of the cities he had traveled with his master. He felt city people forgot their place once they moved out of the bush and outlined areas. It's as if they think living in the city has advanced them somehow along the human evolution chain. Suddenly his own thoughts were interrupted, a stabbing invading pain shot in his head. All he could manage was an "arrgh" sound from his lips. He looked up into the night clutching his head with both of his hands, and shouted, "I'm coming master; give me a few more seconds please!" As quickly as he uttered the words, the pain was gone. Bes felt like someone had just stuck a hot poker in his ear and that his pleadings were the only thing that caused the pain to stop. He began running now, and reaching his destination was top priority, he could not stand another mind probe like that. The few town people that were still mingling around saw the animation of the little man and thought he was just being odd. Karnak seemed to be a haven for odd people lately.

At the western end of the city, the pyramid plateau was visible, like the great plateau built in Giza. It had been said, by the elders here in Karnak, to have been the original concept of the southern plateau but something changed the architect's plans. And it was later built in the south at Giza for another Dynasty. The small city of Karnak was a backdrop to these two magnificent structures, - one the monument to a once great king Menkaure now long dead and forgotten, and the smaller one a tribute to his great queen Nefertari. The old villagers spoke of the old kingdoms with great honor, The Tarharqean age, the Ramesean age, The Thutmosean age and many, many more, but when they speak of the Setetsenra reign the old men go mute, as if the age of that clan interrupted life as they knew it or was too old to recount.

Bes approached the smaller of the two pyramids. The people of this region knew nothing about these ancient structures, he thought. His people were the early developers of these facsimiles. They didn't house the burial remains of any kings or queens. At least not in their inception, these beautiful things were the replicas of the landmarks the Kemetians came from. South of Kemet, at the foothill of the mountain of the moon, this was the sacred land and early, long before the many tribes were born, there were many volcanoes in the land and those pyramids, (as people called them,) were named houses of fire by the Twi. We advised the kings in their building to remind the people of Kemet where their origins began least they forget. What they use them for now, well that's the so-called advances of the city people. He smirked to himself as he remembered the history of these sacred structures. Bes's small stature made navigating in the monument relatively easier than a man twice his size.

As he descended the steps east of the base, the low ceiling and narrow walls made most people uncomfortable as if they were closed in. He reached for a small lantern hanging on the hook of the wall, carefully raising the glass covering the wick; he fished for a match, struck it on the wall and lit the lantern. The illumination was instant and he could see the hallway much clearer than his squinting eyes alone. The sound inside of this passageway was eerie at times, the night winds blowing off of the desert made a faint humming sound that resembled a fading human voice. He continued down in the place until he was several meters under the base of the structure. The air was different here, thinner and old. Bes was not the least bit uncomfortable in this low pressing ceiling and tight space. It was this very condition that kept thieves and the curious away. He pressed an ancient mechanism in the wall known only to those who used it, and the sliding of a great stone began. It moved forward in the room taking up what little space could be maintained and left room for only a man of Bes' origin. If any man taller or larger than him was standing in this room as the mechanism was started the great stone would crush him.

A dim light was emanating from the stone that collapsed as the larger stone above it moved into the room. Bes' head just barely clearing the huge stone above moved towards the light. He called out to someone as he took steps down to this hidden chamber. "Master, it is I, your faithful servant." "Aye and who else would I expect skulking around down here, my little one?" came an echoing answer. Bes looked to the place he knew he would find his benefactor sitting, in a room that appeared to be the crypt of a long buried Kemetian king.

Every imaginable object was in this room piled like discarded antiques. Tables of ancient designs, pots, cups, plates to eat food from. The chariot of a once great warrior wrought in gold, and the finest wood now covered in dust from this settling monument. Fabulously crafted chairs for the once living to sit on. And at the center of all this hoarding sat the most striking piece in the room, a great chair with the typical U shaped arms of the Kemetian period, only exaggerated, to give the appearance of who ever is sitting in the chair to appear to be larger than those standing before them. In such a gold crafted chair sat a man not seen in this time for thousands of centuries.

If you start at his well maintained feet you notice adorned the beautiful sandals, ancient by the modern standards, single toe strap shape like the symbol of the ankh across the instep, and his calves, huge like those of a foot soldier, who had walked many miles to battle. Even with him sitting, you could tell by his long legs he was well over six feet tall. His mass was impressive, and at the lip of the huge seat of the chair, rested his gigantic thighs, pressing at the sides of the chair as if too small to contain them. The pleated linen skirt he wore, with the battle leather lying in the center immediately identified the wearer as a warrior. His arms, ripped with muscles were fearsome, a work of art, his hands strong but elegant. You can see the vascular indentations on the back of the hands as they drape over the arm of the chair, and running all the way to the biceps across the forearms is the same mapping of strength. Without a doubt, his appendages telegraphed the ways of a disciplined person. His midriff is bare and you notice the ripples in his stomach area, even while seated, are defined. His bare chest is only interrupted by the circular collar piece around his shoulder, which is multi-colored, and encrusted in precious stones, covering his entire upper chest and shoulders.

You are now drawn to his face. The sun has kissed his skin pleasantly, not black like the beautiful Nubians and Ethiopians but a shade or two lighter, more like the Masai. There are no tribal scars to be seen on the face, his lips are full and perfect, like the statues of Sesostris I of the 12th dynasty. His nose, slightly protruding from his face, runs straight to his brow without a crooked turn. His cheekbones are high and strong like the Mandinka warriors of the west. When you see his dark eyes, that this dim light cannot do justice to, you are mesmerized. The thing that places this man in a different time is noticed immediately, when you get to his face his head is shaven completely except for his thick eyebrows, your eyes are drawn past his smooth shaved head that is perfectly symmetrical, to the Kemetian side hair lock. Not worn in this region by men any longer. The symbol of youth, the hair has separate braids or locks usually four to nine individual pieces about shoulder length; these locks are then braided into one complete braid with three other sections on the side of the head to form one large unified lock. The wealthy hold the end of the lock with a gold or precious metal clamp.

The striking man looks at Bes. "My wayward little servant, have you good news for me tonight?" he began. Bes quickly fell to his knees and gave obeisance to the figure. "Yes oh great one, I have found him, the one whom you seek." "Well, tell me where is the wayward son of Menkaure," he requested with the tone of unbelief. Bes rose from his knees and began to speak but instead of answering immediately, he began with, "You know I've been thinking, I have served you well these past years and you have promised me to go free, back to my home". The man interrupted Bes' dissertation, leaning forward he asked, "Would you be so foolish as to bargain with me"? Bes completely capitulated, angering this man was not wise and he had learned early on that he was not one to press. The words themselves did not scare Bes but the timbre of them is what brought forth from his mouth quickly. "Yes, true south of the Ausurian star that's his entry way. Just at the end of the town south into the forest." "Good are you certain he didn't see you?" "Oh no, I stayed in the cover of the trees until he vanished into the bush." "Excellent, by tonight I will behold his face again." He stood from the throne chair walked toward the little man; he patted him on the head like a father would his child. "Good work my tiny servant, you go now and meet me at the woods' edge tonight. I must sleep until then." Bes turned to leave and the man he just gave the most important bargaining leverage he had in many years just walked off into the dark of the chamber. He was disappointed but glad he wasn't struck for his insolence. Bes made his way out and thought of his home.

Sarset woke about midday; she saw the room for the first time in the day. It was very pleasant to the eyes and she wondered how Menkaraa came about it. She eased out of the bed and reached for the soft nightgown she had covered herself with during the night. She was anxious to explore the house, but she needed water before she would begin exploring the wonders of the residence. Sarset cautiously opened the bedroom door. She did not want Mister Ku to mistake her for a meal, even if his master said he wouldn't. Relieved that there was only an empty hall outside her door, she stepped out into the huge hallway and made her way in the direction she thought might be the kitchen. The castle was not anything familiar to her, a house this size had to be built by the foreigners who lived in her land now. The wood was handcrafted and rich. The walls were made of stone, smooth and milled. As if who ever had it built wanted to remind themselves of another place not the thatch homes it loomed over. She could see the touches of Menkaraa in the hallways, large murals of ancient places and faces. As she reached the stairway the carving of the railways had more workmanship foreign to her, the wood was reddish almost like cherry, but she didn't know the different types of wood. She just knew it was breath taking, the steps were reflecting her shadow in them even with the slight film of dust that was collecting.

The steps ran steep to the bottom. Sarset stepped carefully holding on with one hand to the fine carved rails, as her feet took noncommittal movements. At the bottom of the great staircase, she looked in the direction left of her and then right, still nothing gave her a hint to the kitchen. The floors led down long corridors and at first they appeared too daunting to walk. She gathered her reserve and took off down to the right of the stairs. The sound of her footsteps was all that she could hear as she searched. Each door along the hall opened to a new experience behind it. Rooms with ancient weapons, a room of statues and busts of people she had heard of in history classes at the small village schools. There was a room that looked like it was intended to hold hand-to-hand combat practice, complete with a soft matted floor and padded walls. Above the padding was graffiti of men wrestling, fencing, and some other combative activity she didn't recognize, adding credence to her feeling that her host practiced his fighting skills in the room.

As she pulled the last door of the hallway closed, the sound of the closing door was loud and echoing. Sarset leaned against the door somewhat exhausted but still determined to find the kitchen or another bathroom, and not wanting to give up after all the walking she had committed to. One door left, just ahead she stood at the threshold of it, swung it open and the flashing of the hanging pots and cookware blinded her as she stepped into the kitchen. A large smile overcame her face and she was impressed by the cleanliness of the large kitchen, it was as if someone kept it so for unexpected guests. Menkaraa she thought, nah he didn't eat food like this anymore or did he? Sarset had her head in one of the cupboards when the sound of a doorknob startled her. She turned to see a large woman burdened down with what looked like a basket of food, squeezing her way into the rear door of the kitchen. Both women exclaimed "Oh" at the same time. "Can I help you with those", Sarset finally asked after the initial surprise. "Ahh no child, I can handle an arm full of market goods." The woman placed the things on the table sighed an air of relief and then turned to Sarset. "Well child, my name's Nanathar, my friends call me Nan, and I am the mistress of this kitchen. What can I get you or fix you?" Her wide smile beamed from a genuine joy of her announced position.

Sarset said, "I'm sorry for intruding into your kitchen, I'm Sarset, I didn't know anyone worked here I've only been a guest for a couple of days, and this has been the first time I journeyed through the house." "Honey don't apologize, I just come by each month and keep the icebox cool, restock the cupboards and clean the kitchen." Nanathar responded as she began to unload the items she brought into the door. Sarset said, "Oh, do you know the owner Menkaraa?" "Men-who? Honey I just go where the foreigners assign work to the domestics in Karnak. You know those bastards don't tell us anything." Sarset was slightly embarrassed at Nan's language; most women in this region did not use abrasive words, but her smile and spirit excused any rugged misspoken words. She continued with, "I thought they just kept this castle up here for when they entertained their guests or some visiting dignitary. I've never seen anyone before you in this house, though I've heard strange sounds but I've never wandered off to see what they were, none of my business child." Sarset liked this woman, she reminded her of her mother's people, strong females with opinions that came to the surface quickly but didn't linger to depress the conversation.

"Well, that's done", Nan announced, as the last item was closed behind the cupboard, "do you want me to get you something eggs, bread, drink?" Sarset said, "water would be fine and could you tell me where the wash room is?" Nan smiled and said, "right over near the closet there", pointing past Sarset's left shoulder. Nan began to pour Sarset her water and lit the top stove to begin preparing breakfast. Sarset exited the washroom and was pleasantly assaulted by the aroma of what Nan was cooking. "Come on child, pull up a chair and eat a good meal, I fixed eggs and strips of pork and fresh morning cakes, they'll be ready in just a few minutes. I brought them this morning from in town all I have to do is warm them." Sarset could not refuse, besides she was famished. She ate until her tummy signaled it was full and pushed the plate away, Nan asked her if she wanted more, and Sarset shook her head quickly and said "not another bite, thank you very much I must take a bath and find the library." "Well I can't help you there, I am under strict orders to not leave the kitchen area I have no idea what is in this house and where it is located."

Sarset looked at the woman as she began the process of cleaning up the plates they just ate off of, and how quickly she took on her responsibilities with no prompting from an overseer. "Well thank you Ms. Nan, the food was delicious and your company refreshing. I leave you to your duties and hope to see you again." "You take care ma'am and come see me again if you are visiting again, bye now." Sarset bidded the woman goodbye and closed the door to the kitchen behind her. The huge hall once again engulfed her and she made her way down the way she had come. Walking back down the hall, Sarset realized she forgot her water, oh well, she knew where the kitchen was and she could make her way back later, maybe Nan would still be there, and they could talk longer. The house was vast; the hallways had multiple doors leading to engaging room after engaging room, as Sarset made her way to the east wing of the mansion. She came upon the desire of her eye, the walls were glass and encased in them were shelf after shelf of books.

When she reached the mid point of the hall, double glass doors opened to the daunting sanctuary. What a beautiful place she thought standing in the midst of the room. Wherever she turned, she saw books and the path of the hall she came down. In the room were selective pieces of furniture. A sled-like chair that invited the reader to sit and read comfortably, even pillows to prop against the back. Two well-placed hand made chairs that were made from the scraps found in any woods, the branches bound together by rope and fashioned into a deep-seated circle. The pillows softened the rugged look the hand made chairs had. "Well" Sarset said out loud, "what shall I find to read?" Her fingers lightly skimmed the spines of the books on the shelves. She relished the eclectic mix, books of monarchs, kingdoms, wars, folklore, biographies, philosophies; they went on endlessly she knew not where to begin. Her eyes then fell on a most curious book. "The Purging's", she was curious and pulled the book from the shelf. It was an old leather bound cover with what appeared to be papyrus paper as its text.

She perused it and came across the author's name Menkaraa 9th son of Menkaure, he whom Ra had cursed and brought about the fall of the house of Setetsenra. The words went on about a clash between men and Ausar. She decided she would take this book back to her room and read more. Could this be what Menkaraa meant running from his father's past, this clash? Sarset was tired; the library was too much, too many books to browse. She wanted to bathe and explore this book more. She wasn't certain if Menkaraa would mind her bringing the book along with her but she told herself, he wouldn't mind.

Sarset closed the door to her room the water bucket was somewhat heavy hauling all the way from the kitchen. Nan was no longer there, but she left a plate of delicious looking cookies with a note, "Sarset, child I enjoyed our meeting this afternoon, thought you might like a little snack take care now Nan". She liked that woman; the bonds between women in this country were strained because of all the incursions in this region from foreign people. Families were destroyed with the slave trade, and raping of the natural resources. It was as if the indigenous people of Karnak never lived here and raised families and had a life they called their own. Sarset sighed, and began to heat her water for her bath, she sat in the chair that was familiar since talking with Menkaraa and opened the book she borrowed from the library.

CHAPTER NINE

An entry began: In the year 5252 b.c.e. (before the common era) great dread has fallen upon Waset city of my family. I have been taken capture after witnessing a most grisly act, my father Menkaure sire of Kemet has changed into a monster, they hold me here, in this chamber so that I cannot speak on, or hear or see the things taking place in our home. My brother is in this space with me. They feed us and they continue to allow our tutoring and growing. I have not seen our older brothers in days. If they were near they would release us from the wrong of this imprisonment. Sarset knew that this was Menkaraa writing about some wrong that had befallen him, but how old is he at this writing, and which brother is imprisoned with him, and how could this be taking place in the year indicated, and Menkaraa be alive now in 1341 a.c.e.?

Sarset closed the book and began to prepare for her bath. The creaking of Menkaraa's door was reaching his ears as a familiar sound, in the approaching darkness he spoke his name "Ku", the low growl of the lion pierced the darkness. "We just can't agree on the sanctity of this room", Menkaraa stood and smiled at the persistence of the lion. He was pensive he wondered how Sarset faired during the day. He had not slept well and actually if it were possible he had a nightmare. His uneasiness upon rising did not subside and was like a heavy damp outer cloak, weighing down on him, aching to be removed. The images first came as choppy, vague, flashing in his mind erratically at first. He saw his family bound and about to be destroyed, a fire of immense proportions rising to the sky as if it would consume the heavens, the heat he felt even in his vampiric state of unconsciousness. His family appeared to be pleading to a stoic-faced man that he could not make the features out clearly. The heat, the screams, the look upon his mother's face, these ruptured his rest. He gathered a change of clothing; some things in his life had not changed. When he left his lair and fed there was a stench and uncleanness he felt and he bathed at times in the waters of the lakes and rivers. A human characteristic some might say that he had not put off. Creatures like Menkaraa had a slight odor to them, they are quite dead and the animation of life that they possess is precariously situated in death. Moreover, he faintly felt at times like a rotten corpse, a dead thing. Menkaraa made his way to the door of his lair. He would allow Ku to hunt on his own tonight and leave the stone rolled away for his return.

Bundle in hand; he sprung upward like a great falcon. Ku roared beneath him at the suddenness of his ascent. Menkaraa landed with the sound of disturbed grass under foot, looked back over his shoulder down at the majestic beast and murmured, "You'll find your way." He stepped through the brush that hid the drop to his haven. The forest was alive and his senses quickly consumed the familiar. Owls hooting in the cool of the covering, small vermin running in the brush, he could even hear the night snakes slithering in the grass.

Menkaraa had his own rules for the hunt. The elderly were never a prey, nor small children who had not had a chance to begin to live a life. Never would he bite a female for nourishment, although there were some he was tempted to, because he wanted to possess them and feel the wonder of their femininity that might have captivated him. Sarset was such a beauty but he had long relinquished the idea of defiling her. He felt she belonged in this time and life, free as a human. His pondering is interrupted for a moment; the house of Sarset and her parents is in the clearing. It's as if without thought or purposes his feet had walked him to this familiar place. Oh well, he thought, let me look in on Sarset's parents. The girl had best taken care of them Menkaraa thought.

Menkaraa could hear voices coming from the house as he got closer, and immediately he heard a man's voice and the girl he hired, and the presence of another. Menkaraa dropped his bundle beside the tree and walked like an invisible wraith to the front door, changing his appearance and clothing as he went. When he knocked on the door the voices inside went silent. He was intrigued now and pulled his cloak up over his head as he waited for someone to answer. A voice pierced through the door, "Yeah what do you want?" Menkaraa now knew that something was wrong. The voice was not Sarset's father and it sounded like the voice of a brutal man. He responded to the voice with "Is Lela in?" "No, she's gone for the night". "Would you happen to know where?" "Look, Lela's not here so get going be on your way". Menkaraa's hand came through the door where the man stood, dematerialized at first then solid when it clamped across his mouth. The rest of his body began to dematerialize and become solid on the other side of the door as he stepped into the house. "Quiet", is all he spoke in the trembling man's ear, "where are your two friends?" He pointed to the hallway where the bedroom of Sarset's parents was. He slammed the villain against the beam of the hallway and felt him go limp on the floor. "Jahe, Jahe, the voice came again is everything ok?" Menkaraa recognized the voice of the girl. He was a great mimicker; he had heard the voice of the unconscious villain enough to imitate it. "I'm all right, just knocked over this lamp, the fool is gone."

He searched for the name of the other person in the room with Lela, there it is. "You and Kabal meet me in the kitchen, the old ones will not move." He drug the unconscious man by his foot like a slaughtered animal and waited. Obediently they walked into the kitchen and Menkaraa snatched them both up by their throats. Dangling in midair like struggling lifeless puppets. The woman pleaded for mercy. "They made me, they forced me to show them to this place", she gagged out. "I warned you woman to entreat these old ones with respect. You have taken my warning lightly and that is unforgiving." Kabal was struggling in Menkaraa's grasp trying to reach for his knife. He drew the helpless man to his mouth and bit down hard almost to the bone the sound made Lela faint right away. The blood rushed to his heart and swam through his body. He dropped the body of the woman unto Jahe's unconscious form and enraptured himself in the meal. The completion of the drink left three bodies lying on top of each other. He looked down at the pile and drug all three by their legs out the kitchen door. He wiped the blood from his mouth and returned to the hallway. He adjusted his clothing and knocked on the door, "Ms. Tuya are you okay?" He opened the door and found the two elders sitting on the bed. The woman was nursing the old man who had received a blow to the head. "Yes, young man I'm okay. My husband has been mistreated but we are fine." Menkaraa let her know that the men responsible had been removed and that they should hear from Sarset by morning.

As he walked toward the door to leave, he turned back and said, "Lela will not be returning, I'll try to find a replacement more suitable if your daughter is delayed any longer, goodnight". He was once again in the dark of the night. He enjoyed these little skirmishes; they gave him a sense of being alive of having purpose and meaning. He always hunted the undesirables. Not because they were any more vile than the next creature, but just because there were so many of their kind. They moved in the night in the shadow of the moon. Preying on the weak and defenseless beings as if they were fodder for their all consuming appetite. He ate them where he found them, in the small villages stealing animals or in the taverns hustling some one in a game of chance, or the seedy places of vice and whoredom. In Africa, Asia, Europe, the undesirables are spread all over this world, for a creature like himself to feast and hunt.

Menkaraa took no thought of their lives because they had no mercy on their marks. He never listened to their pleadings or their screams, it was irrelevant, and the chain of command on this planet had shifted to him being at the top of the food chain. Enough, he thought these musings were consuming his night. He would wash in the river Aur, or the Nile as these invaders renamed it. This amused him, as he dragged the bodies of the fools that preyed on Sarset's parents. The idea that other people possess a land after a formal tenant and change the names of the rivers, the cities, and origins of the place. These new people were strange; their endless appetite of the land, people and resources reminded him of the voracity of a vampire. How ironic! He feasted on the men of war, the officials of states, men of substance, people who bartered the lives of whole nations. With great impunity he would dispatch a judge, a military official a soldier any and all that kept the wound of humanity open and festering.

Menkaraa, the vampire that sucked the blood of the vampires of humanity, which made him laugh as he tossed the bodies of the woman and men in a ravine hidden deep in the bush, the drop from this height would finish the two he had not drank from. Running now almost not touching the ground with his feet, he snatched up his bundle from the tree and felt his locks brush the branches of the trees as he took flight, he could hear the rivers flow growing close as he reached the bank, dropping the clothes he removed his clothes in mid air and began to descend at great speed towards the water's clear moving surface. When his hands pierced the water the engulfing water overcame his intrusion and slowed his fall and pressed him back to the surface. Menkaraa did not need to inhale air in water; his supernatural form defied the intrinsic laws of this world. He was flexing now, the water made his body feel somewhat alive.

Though it was dark he swam under the surface reaching and pulling the water out the way to propel his form forward. The water was the only element that seems to recognize his existence. Fire took great stoking to tax him. Air was needed and yet not needed, and the earth could be overcome with the slightest manipulation. The one element he missed was Ra (sun) it did not tolerate his existence. If it caught a glimpse of his flesh it would burn. It held him captive in darkness with no possible appeal. In his human life the sun was worshipped and adored. With each rising the people welcomed its warmth and perpetual life-giving caress. He was now a fugitive and vagabond of Ra. He made for the surface and rose above the waters, the water dripped from his limbs and his hair hung wet and heavy on his head. He turned like a frozen object above the water until he saw the bundle of clothes. From the center of the Aur river to the bundle was a mere thought. He dressed and felt cleansed from the first part of his night's opposition, not like a dead thing but as his mind searched for the right word – human, he felt human.

CHAPTER TEN

Bes was making his way to the edge of the forest. He knew that being late could be the wrong way to start the night off with his master. As he drew near the woods edge he heard voices, the voice of a female and two men seemingly arguing. Bes walked carefully towards their bickering, trying not to be seen or heard he was closer now. Drawing back the hidden foliage he saw them a young Arab/African mixed woman, standing in front of two imposing Arab men. She was pleading with them about some old couple. "Look Jahe, I will show you where the old ones live, but I think you should not engage the stranger that hired me." "Woman make your tongue still, I care not for these old ones you speak about. I want the man that paid you in gold coins and those old ones must know who he is." "Jahe", the woman urged him "he did not appear to be from here and he spoke like no man I've known. He warned me to treat them well and not to bring harm to them." "Lela shut your mouth", the other man spoke, "Jahe and I can handle any strange black foolish enough to come here paying with gold coins." Lela snapped her head around to the man, "No, you shut up Kabal, you will get Jahe and I killed with your greed and want."

Their bickering humored Bes, and he wondered who had threatened the girl in such a way that she would engage two gruff men. He watched the threesome, walk off into the brush, the girl trying to pull her arm out of the clutch of her companions. The advantage of his Twi stature allowed him such unexposed views of private conversations and hidden exchanges; he was fascinated by the drama, but not enough to miss his destination with the formidable brooding prince. He was unsure of his present temperament and patience. Just as Bes felt the thoughts leave his consciousness, he stepped into an unmovable object. The thudding sound of his small body colliding into the legs of his master startled him. "Ohhhh, I was. Was on my way sir", he stammered from his lips. The man reached down and lifted him by the nape of his shirt and drew him up to his eye level. "Are you quite done wasting time in the cover of these woods?" The Twi nodded his head in silence. He was afraid of his master, and for good reason. "Good, then let us proceed to this entrance you saw." Bes's legs and arms dangled like a clipped marionette as the prince made his way through the wooded terrain at the urgings and directions of his hapless servant.

Menkaraa was in the hallway now, he was thinking of Sarset and what the night's conversation would be, he had opened up to her, she was easy to speak with like a trusted friend listening to his every intimate thought. Besides, she was such an attractive sight, that her beauty captivated him; his constant speaking only serving at times to superficially disguised his admiration and temptation to just stare at her as he had done so in the woods many times. He approached her room, and almost instinctively dematerialized through the door without announcing his presence. Pausing momentarily, he remembered how she previously chastised him for breaching her thoughts. Menkaraa was sort of amused at this new etiquette he now employed to engage her, never before, in his vampire life had he limited his behavior to no one or no thing.

He tapped on her door, and spoke her name, "Sarset are you awake?" The voice breaching the solid door eased softly to his hears, "Yes, give me a minute", it was obvious that he had caught her finishing up her grooming, and Sarset in all her humbleness was still vain about a man seeing her before she had completed the appearance ritual that all females indulged themselves in. "Do you wish for me to come back in a moment?" "Oh no, here I come." The door opened and like sun pouring into a window her face beamed at him. "Good evening Sarset, have you slept well? Has your day been eventful?" He did not probe her mind for answers as before, he waited for her response. "Come in Menkaraa, yes, I have had quite an eventful day." He looked about her room and could feel her feminine warmth engulfing it. The room seemed to enjoy her stay, and there was a kind of vibrancy to the typically stale air of the chamber.

Menkaraa sat down and Sarset walked after him and seated herself across from him, he exuded the very essence of a royal demeanor. Her thoughts on the power of his presence, he interrupted. "Have you read much?" The question startled her at first then she noticed he was looking at the book she laid down on the small table face down. I hope you don't mind my perusing it and taking it from the library." "No, just some memories of long ago, things that I try not to recall any more. I once thought I should keep a record, in fact I began it as a chronicle to assuage my hours of isolation." "Is this true in the passage that your father and Bak literally imprisoned you and your brother?" "Well that is a little harsh, but those are the words of a twelve year old and I was frightened at first. You see Sarset, my father and his most trusted friend had a vision. A vision that many would not have engaged, they would not have the timber or the stomach for such an undertaking.

The tears of a sorrowful king are an unusual sound to hear. Rarely do leaders of kingdoms express emotion for any decisions they have rendered. My father sat in the chair with Bak in his lap and wept. Just as he stared at the unmoving body of his friend, Mother had returned to the door, and my father ordered her to leave his presence, he consoled her telling her that they would speak later. The body of my fathers, beloved Bak just lay there, staring back at him, once full of life, but now limp yet his eyes seem to be saying look what you have done. Well like all great men, my father gathered himself and stood at the window of his chamber. He wiped the drying tears from his eyes and began to run the worst scenario of this curse on his bloodline. He thought, the people could find out and he would be hunted and killed, or the horde of Kemet's enemies would find out that they are without a leader and strike at her while she was weak. "Neither sire," the voice was familiar but shallow. Menkaure turned to the sound of it, and standing on his feet before him, stood Bak. "Not surprised to see me are you my Lord?" "Bak", "No need to apologize sire, you did what you thought best". Bak said reassuringly to my father. "I must admit this vestige of my formal self is quite intriguing. I feel much younger than my previous eighty years. It is as if Ausar himself has given me life anew like in our folklore. Sarset interrupted "Ausar, who is that?" Menkaraa looked at Sarset and asked her, "do your people know anything about this land before the white Northerners, Greek, and Arabs came?" "Very little" she sheepishly responded, "we have been governed and oppressed for so long that the elders are no longer alive to speak the tale."

Menkaraa agreed. Then I shall tell you about the legend of Ausar and Auset. Ausar is known as the god of transformation and immortality; he is also called the king of the dead. In his human state he was Lord of creation, he became king of Kemet and taught the people science and husbandry, he instituted a moral code of laws. He brought to Kemet peace and prosperity, and in his reign he began to journey out and teach other nations. In his absence, the great wife queen Auset ruled Kemet. Unfortunately like all rulers in Kemet there were his detractors, those who wished to rule with iron hands and closed minds. Set his brother from the North, was jealous of Ausar and conspired to entrap and slay him. Knowing of his absence he came to the Queen Auset and asked her if he could help in the celebration of the imminent return of the king. She wished not to offend Set so she asked what could he offer to the celebration. Set said he would entertain the guest of the king with a new game for the court. Auset agreed and excused him from the audience.

Now Auset advisors warned the queen not to trust Set, that he had been seen in the company of his brother's enemies. She replied that she saw no way without offending her husband's brother to deny him participation. So as the tale is told Ausar returned from his sojourning and the feast for his return began. All was joyous and happy. Set stood and offered a salutation to his brother Ausar. "May the reign of my beloved brother continue and the peace of Kemet be eternal." Ausar thanked Set and the people gathered, and then he asked to see the new amusement Set had provided for today's festivities. At the handclap of Set, the hall went silent. The great doors slowly creaked open and eight men bared the weight of a bejeweled stone box. The audience was awe struck and many had never seen such an object carried by men before. As the gold laid box and jewel studded object made its way through the hall, the people touched it with their hands in admiration. The men halted and sat the box in the center of the gathering. Set said gather children of Kemet this box you behold is the chamber and owner of the god who can fit its exact dimensions.

There is only one who can fit in the box perfectly, the men drew it from the Aur River itself and the Gods would have the owner claim it. The people laughed and clamored, they surely would try to claim such an exquisite prize. "Let me try" a countryman said and tried as he could, he did not fit in the box. The laughter was deafening and the people were enjoying this game of Set's. As the last of the people tried to fit into the jeweled box, Set looked to the king Ausar and said, "Oh great father of Kemet none of your children can claim the prize from the gods. Perhaps the gift is from the gods to the king himself. Ausar looked upon his brother, it is not befitting for a king to participate in such gratuitous revelry. Ahh brother it is merely a game, if the gift is for you, give it to a deserving servant in your house or among the assembly. The people cried in unison "Yes yes, play the game and honor one in your service." Ausar raised his hand and quieted the guest. I shall play the game this once only because my brother is the author of its introduction to us. With that Ausar stood and walked to the box, he stepped into the entrance, right hand, right leg first and turned his back to its bottom, his head fitting perfectly, and as he situated his body perfectly in place. Suddenly Set sprung forward and slammed the lid closed on Ausar. Auset screamed out and Set's men rushed the box and sealed the latches that held it shut.

Set spoke to the assembled; this day brings to an end the chapter of Ausar's reign. The people will now follow me and the dynasty of the north shall rule all of Kemet from this day forth, is there any that wish to speak out against this decision? Auset spat, "Oh wicked and treacherous Set I will not adhere to such madness." "Well besides the former queen, is there anyone else that does not approve? Good, bare the box up and out of this place."

Set's men hoisted the box up and out of the room to the cries and silence of the people. Auset ran towards the imprisoned Ausar and the guards that once defended her beloved Ausar, now took orders from Set. They led her in the other direction of her entrapped beloved. They say the tears of Auset were like the seasonal flood of the river Aur, in fact the annual flooding is in remembrance of the treachery of Set that day, and the weeping of the beautiful Auset.

Meanwhile the men of Set took the box to the river's edge. The airless seal had caused Ausar to slip into unconsciousness; the men opened the lid and at Set's command cut Ausar into 13 pieces. His feet and then at his knees his thighs, phallus and lower waist, his hands and arms and his head. All the portions they tossed into the river so that the water would carry his remains away. Auset lamented the death of Ausar, and in her grief she sought the pieces of her murdered husband. She felt even the treachery of Set could not destroy the life of Ausar. She eventually found all the pieces of Ausar and began to reassemble them. The reanimation of Ausar was like that of any ghoul or vampire. He was a dead thing not alive and not dead, suspended between the realm of the living and the passed. He became the King of the dead. He wept with his wife but told her he could not return to the day. "I must go to the underworld, there my beloved kingdom lies. I will give you a gift before I go, one that will rise from you and slay the evil of Set. Auset begged him and wept not to leave her, he embraced her and comforted her. "Auset in you I have given you the future of Kemet. Raise your son and he will raise Kemet. And so as Heru is the son of the reborn Ausar and his wife Auset, so are all the god kings of Kemet descended."

It is this tale that sparked the idea of Bak." Sarset entreated "what idea?" "You see my dear" Menkaraa began. Bak saw the parallel in the resurrected Ausar and this vampire state. "My king you are the risen Ausar, like him you cannot see the light of Ra again, and like him you are the Lord of the dark." "How can I rule Kemet from the dark my faithful friend?" my father asked. "That sire is not a real problem, it is the other affairs of Kemet we must be able to navigate. You are not seen in public much sire, and we can move the affairs that need your direct intervention to dusk." "What of my family, Nefertari, my sons? How do I explain this blood curse, this evil?" Menkaure was asking the questions as if he was being interrogated for a crime not yet committed. My king these are real issues for you and Kemet, but we are blessed with an opportunity here that your fathers and his father have not been offered, remember the demon said to you. "You will suck the blood of other humans and you will grow to despise them, you will either destroy this kingdom or yourself; neither really matters to creatures such as us." We can raise this kingdom up, so that it is the envy of the entire world. Not just now in our day, but for all eternity," Bak pleaded. "Other kings have failed for one reason and one reason only." "What is that Bak?" Bak walked over to his dejected monarch; standing in front of Menkaure he said the words slowly. "My lord they died. They died, without ever seeing their hard work and plans fulfilled. They died, and their children squandered the fortune they

Khpra Senwosret

accumulated and did not follow through with the vision. You my lord are the first of your line that is the true personification of Ausar, a risen king, God of the dead."

Menkaure began to see what his friend was telling him. "Yes, Bak an interesting idea. We will use this gift, this advantage to subdue our enemies and we won't need the strength of the priest clans or their superstitions. Kemet will herald in the age of the everlasting dynasty. I will sit on its throne and we shall never be removed." Menkaraa looked at Sarset. "I don't know to this day if my father asked my mother, or my older brothers if they wanted to be a part of this madness or if he just violated them and made them a part of his new blood family. I do know that he handled my brother and I differently, as I struggled in the arms of Bak, he implored me to be still, to calm down. I couldn't, I just saw the woman I loved with all my heart being attacked by the man I once respected above all men. Let go, let go of me I told him, what has father done to mother?" "It is not for you to know the plans of your father, come with me and, his words were interrupted."

Like a child I kicked him in his shins trying to extricate myself from his grasp. "My prince this is futile," he snatched me up by the collar of my nightshirt and walked with my body held out at his side. I dangled and squirmed all the way, screaming "let me down, let me go!" Awaiting me was a holding chamber of sorts, not a room or a closet,

106

just a closed area empty and quiet. I looked about to try to see where in our home this place was but I never had seen such an empty space. Our sleeping quarters were always indulged with objects and furnishings. The great artists of our time painted the walls with murals of beautiful colors and scenes. This place is desolate, I thought, as is my heart.

My overwhelmed young mind slipped into sleep and the resisting steps of my new companion being placed in this holding place awakened me. The royal guards of my father's court had Seti by his arms on either side and tossed him roughly through the door. "Seti, are you all right?" "Bother not for me little one attend to your own fears." Sarset interjected, "who is Seti and why is he so abrupt, to you?" The question reached Menkaraa like a furlong love letter; he stood from his chair and searched for the words. Sarset's eyes followed his form and stayed fixed on his movement. When he came to a pause at the window the light of the moon lit his face and she could see he was struggling. He gathered himself and sat in the window's sill crossed his arms and said, "Seti, is my fathers Set. If he believed himself to be the risen Ausar then my brother Seti became Set. Menmare Seti Setetsenra is the eight son of Menkaure he was a loner from birth, it was believed that he was my father's lesser wife's child, I was not concerned with who his mother was as a child, he was my brother, not part, not half, but blood of our blood. Until the age of ten he was not concerned either, it wasn't until we over heard the servants while playing say that he was a prince that never could sit on the throne did things change. I watched my brother go solemn. From that day forward he no longer played with me, he stayed in his chamber studying and brooding.

I would ask mother to entreat him and implore him to come out of his room. She simply said "Let him be little prince, Menmare has grown up and no longer seeks play." I never accepted that, I felt Seti was my friend not just my brother and I intruded on him at every moment and many times his response to my intrusion was a flung book or a witty retort. "Go away little worm before I eat you!" I did not care as long as he spoke if only for that second and the engagement was my only desire."

CHAPTER ELEVEN

As they drew near the entrance, the stranger dropped Bes harshly to the ground. The grass and broken twigs crackled beneath him, and he managed a grumble from his lips at his ill treatment. The prince only looked down and Bes pointed to the brush. "Is it here you saw him enter?" "Yes" Bes replied. He was about to step forward when he sensed something in the dark. "Wait" he said to his diminutive aide, there is something in the bush. He was trying to get a fix on it but it was still, yet he still smelled it. He stepped into the clearing and the drop caught him off guard for a moment. Bes was right behind him and began to scream for his life, "Hellll-p I will die from this height save me master." The stranger landed with a thud and looked up and caught his falling aide in his arms. Bes sighed with relief and asked, "Where are we?" "We are at his sleep chamber, he answered.. "Who would sleep this far beneath the earth?" "A being you are not familiar with little one." As the words came out in the dark of the tunnel a low growl was heard overhead. Bes looked up where the sound was coming from and said, "What's that, is that the sound of what lives here?" "Yes, I'm sure it lives here but it has a companion the one I seek." Bes could hear the thing ascending upon them and began to recognize the growl as that of a male lion. He said fearfully "sir that is the sound of a lion and lions don't live underground. What shall we do?" "We, my small insignificant friend, what will you do?" Bes reached out as he saw his form dissipate beside him, the lion was on him and the scream never left his mouth.

Suddenly the window where Menkaraa sat speaking to Sarset exploded, the glass and wood frame spewed into the room like a gusting storm. Menkaraa fell forward like an impaled fighter, who was struck from the back by an invisible foe. The glass and wood sprayed the room, and as the impact settled. Menkaraa rose from the suddenness of the attack instinctively, shaking the broken glass off his being; he looked to Sarset and asked, "Are you all right." Sarset curled in the chair shielding herself from the debris barely uttered, "yes what was that?"

The voice boomed in the room "Not what female, who? I am Menmare Seti, brother to that sniveling creature on the floor." Beginning to form out of the dust of the debris was a man levitating just slightly above the floor as if he did not allow his feet to touch the earth. He had on what appeared to be battle armor made of black and tanned leather, it covered the upper body and shoulders and stopped at the plate of stomach muscles that appeared to be rigorously trained. His hips wore a similar linen skirt knotted in the front in some foreign ancient way. His sandals that did not touch the floor bared a symbol that was familiar to her but she couldn't remember where she had seen it, when her eyes looked upon his face his eyes and thick eyebrows fixed her sight, he looked every bit as fierce as he projected. The single lock that braided on the side and fell to his scapula deceived you into thinking you were looking at a young soul. She just could make out the handle of a beautiful crafted sword strapped to his back.

Menkaraa stood there looking at his brother, time had not seemed to move at all from being imprisoned as children to looking at each other in this room. He still degraded him verbally at each possible opportunity. "Sarset move closer to me" Menkaraa implored." "Don't do that creature; I will dictate who moves in this room not him." Seti pointed at Menkaraa while simultaneously baring his fangs at Sarset with a low growl. This had the desired effect for Sarset; she was now frozen in the chair with her eyes wide looking transfixed at Seti. Menkaraa was not frozen, he leaped at his brother and the force of his tackle took them out through the hole that was once his window. Seti got his bearing back as the attack from Menkaraa forced them out of the room and twisted in mid air and wrestled Menkaraa from around his midsection. They both levitated above ground and Seti spoke, "I see you have found some courage in your wanderings brother. We can talk or we can continue this, I looked long for you and not so that you can assault me so." Menkaraa inhaled a breath and spit out, "you assaulted me first with your grand entrance through my now decimated window." Seti looked at him and then suddenly burst out in laughter. "You are right let us begin over and sit and talk.

"What is it you have to say brother, say it here, now, I have other things to tend to." 'The pretty one inside, are you going to feast on her?" "That is not your concern, and don't think to harm her, she is a friend of mine." "You are friends with your food!" "She is not food Seti, and don't refer to her as so," Menkaraa fired back. Seti raised his hands in surrender "as you wish little one. But don't presume that you can tell me what I can do." He pressed the palm of his hand to the chest of his brother as he was drifting past him back towards the window. Seti smiled at Menkaraa, Menkaraa pulled his hand from his chest and continued toward the open hole of his guest bedroom. His feet touched down in the room and Sarset stood. "Are you okay?" "I am fine are you okay, did any of the debris harm you?" Before Sarset could respond Seti appeared back in the room. "Well brother introduce me to this lovely vision." Menkaraa looked at Seti as if he was bothered by the request,

"Sarset this is my brother Menmare Seti Setetsenra, Seti this is the lovely Sarset Mwesea." The brother walked towards Sarset and looked into her eyes, she stood still not knowing exactly what to expect from the being. He reaches for her hand and clasped it in his, Sarset felt a cool palm almost cold, touch her hand he drew it to his lips and kissed it. "I am honored lady, and I must admit rare beauty is seldom seen in this area any longer." He turned to Menkaraa, "she looks much like mother, and they could be sisters. Shall we talk?"

Menkaraa surveyed his brother, he had not aged, a sign that he had been taking good care of himself and feeding well. "Not here Seti, let's retire to one of the dining areas. I'm sure Sarset is hungry." The three walked through the hall as if they were cordial acquaintances, Menkaraa leading the way with Sarset in between the two brothers. As they approached the top of the grand stairs, the cry of Ku was heard. The cat saw Seti and instinctively began to charge the stairs. Sarset gasped and stepped back Menkaraa only spoke, "Ku be still." The male lion paused and roared at Seti, Menkaraa looked at his brother "He must have seen you before it appears he doesn't like you. We met briefly at the entrance to your underground chamber." "And how did you find that?" "An associate of mine that was with me followed you." "And where is he?" Seti simply said, "ask your lion", and he began to descend the stairs past Ku to the bottom. Menkaraa simply looked at his brother still brash and resentful. He looked to Sarset "come my dear, Ku will not harm you" and they walked to the bottom and continued to the dining area with Ku sulking behind them, but keeping an animal's eye on Seti.

Sarset did not enter the dining area she headed for the kitchen hoping to find some food cooked or bought by Nan. Menkaraa began the conversation, "How have you faired brother since the war you declared on the house of my father and yours?" I was young brother and full of anger and despair, unlike you the throne of Kemet was an impossible reality. No half son can set upon it." "You were not a half son to father and you were not a half brother to me", Menkaraa answered, annoyed. "Besides Seti you were eighth of a line of brothers who all could sit on the throne." "Point taken", Seti responded. "I think the transformation changed me, after seven years of tutoring and being confined I resented them." Seti's words caused Menkaraa to slip away in his memory, back to the holding place him and Seti occupied until the footsteps of his Father and his mother and Bak approached. Instinctively, Menkaraa bolted towards his parents. "Mother, Father, what is going on? Why is Seti and I held in this forsaken place?" Menkaraa's youthful eyes searching theirs for an answer, but there was no response.

Menkaure spoke, "my son we have determined that this is a better fate for you and Seti. We have a plan for our home that you two are too young to be involved." Menkaraa tried to interrupt his words, "but father". His father's stern eyes let the words fall short. "You my youngest son must listen to the counsel of your king. Quarters are being built for you and Seti now, and they will be befitting the needs of a prince of Kemet. All will be explained to you by your scribes and instructors."

Nefertari stepped forward, her warm face and gentle voice somewhat unfamiliar at first, "yes my darling prince you will be accorded all you need and well protected. "And who, or whom shall we be protected from?" Seti asked sardonically. Bak spoke this time; the king will have greater enemies than before, those who will try to stop his plans through means of harming you and your little brother. Menkaraa watched the trio they moved differently somehow, his mother would not get closer than a body breath, and his father only stared curiously at them, like a falcon would small prey. Menkaraa wanted to weep, but his father's hard glances kept him from succumbing to his youthful fears. "Will we see you and our brothers often?" asked Menkaraa. Bak spoke this time, "little prince have no fear of these things you will see the entire house of Setetsenra daily. The teachers and aides that will look over you will meet your every need and want." "Mother, Father", Menkaraa implored; "I need you, not servants of the kingdom." The words caused silence to prevail for a moment, and Menkaure broke it as quickly as a hammer would precious glass. "Enough, you my prince will do as we have ordered and you will grow strong and wise and learn later that we have done what is best for you and Seti."

"Father", Seti spoke this time. "I am not interested like Menkaraa here; in will I see you or anyone else? I am a prince of this household and I refuse to be confined or held." "Insolent pup", Bak's words shot at Seti, "the words spoken here are law and what the king has spoken will be adhered to. You will hold your tongue or be." "Or be what? Bak, do we beat the princes of Kemet now or is our fate much worse than that?" This conversation is futile and words are being exchanged that will neither change your lot nor give you understanding, let it go for now fair prince." Nefertari's words silenced Seti, and he turned his back to father and Bak. Bak rushed to speak, but my Father touched his shoulder, shaking his head for him to let it be. My mother looked to me and said "be well sweet prince tomorrow will bring new challenges, and you will learn in time that only your best was thought of in this endeavor." With that they turned in unison like some holy unbreakable trinity, and moved back into the shadow of the hall.

Menkaraa was jarred back into the room, with Seti looking at him in wonderment. "You can't let go can you brother? The mere mention of them takes you away like a lovesick suitor." "I loved them Seti unlike you, I understand what they tried to do." "Oh you do, tell me young one, becoming a vampire is that your idea of a plan well done?" "You chose Seti, I did not, in fact you wanted to be a soul-less thing." Not soulless brother, I have plenty of soul I think the word you are looking for is dead. I am quite that, but my soul is intact and very gregarious." "Yes your fondness for the company you keep is what I question." Seti appeared shocked at the assault of the words, "you mean the priests clan? I only used them Menkaraa, and when I got what I wanted I discarded them as I did…" He seemed hesitant at the last words. "Say it", Menkaraa implored him, "say father and mother." I did not mean to see them die", Seti said with his head lowered. "No, you only facilitated their death." Menkaraa shot back. "And now brother why are we here, why have you sought me out, is it for your dog clan or is there some other sinister plot you have hatched?" The air was affected by the question; it appeared heavier and thick now.

Seti stood pushing the chair back away from his form, he looked to Menkaraa and clenched his fist, and his incisor teeth sprang to the forefront of his mouth as his fist rose above his head. "You are a damnable creature little brother." As those words expelled from his crowded mouth, his hand came crashing down on the table, the impact was such that the splintering wood spewed all over the room as the table could not bear the force. Menkaraa stood quickly bracing for whatever Seti's anger was about to demonstrate. The answer was interrupted by Sarset's appearance. She came through the door bearing a tray of food she had gathered from the kitchen. "Have I missed something," she asked as she looked at Menkaraa then to Seti. In unison they both looked at her and said "nothing my dear." Menkaraa finished the sentence "Just brothers catching up on old times." "Good I wish to know all there is to know about the two of you and your family." They watched her as she moved to the table, placing the tray among them.

Menkaraa as usual loved to watch her movements; he acknowledged the gestures with a slight smile to make her at ease. "Seti do you eat any of the things I have brought from the kitchen?" "No" his voice carrying a tone that was somewhat annoyed. He caught himself and applied a smile to his face, inflecting in his tone an air of superficial kindness. "My dear my appetite is one that moves along the line of those things that are not desirable. Though I must admit I gained a most modest palate." He turned to Menkaraa, "brother I actually drink the blood of common folk." Menkaraa only stared at him; he was neither surprised nor shocked at his brother's comment. Seti was always manipulating the moment and he heard the undertone of an arrogant prince who was trying to slight a poor village girl. He looked to Sarset and she was unfazed by his remark, so he moved on. "So Seti tell us, tell me, why are you here in my humble house?" Seti started with an inhalation of air, "Well I have been bothered of late, and in my travels and experience I have seen the worst of these creatures and the attempts at their best."

"And by creatures who are you referring to Seti, humans whose clan we once belonged, or the new clan of the moving dead?" "Don't get me wrong, I care nothing for this animated food, they are just a meal and a needed necessity. I speak of our ex countrymen. The men who once ruled over a great nation have fallen to their knees and are at the mercy of ignorant tomb raiders. I have watched in amazement how the foreigners have come in and claimed the land, destroyed the buildings and monuments. Defecating on all that is unique and special about this place."

The laughter startled Seti, he paused and looked at Menkaraa, who was now fully beside himself. "Stop, stop" Menkaraa implored, "surely brother you are not suggesting that you Seti the rejected prince of Kemet is looking to correct some wrong on this planet. You are the harbinger of deceit and cunning trickery." "You wound me to the flesh Mens, I am attempting to walk in new sandals that no longer carry the dust of time long past." "Seti this is me your roommate, in our parents and national vizier's self contained camp for those not ready for the kiss. I watch you grow each day and manipulate every lesson taught and every mistake our caretakers made. You honestly expect me to take you seriously. About some humane conversion that you say, you have come to. "Brother your words insult me, I am a creature born to the night, but not last night!" Seti responded immediately to the charge, "I understand that we have history together brother, but you can't see from your prejudice that I too can come to some sanity or peace." "You're absolutely right I can't see that, for the ancestor's sake, let's not forget that you destroyed my father and mother. Am I to forget the pact you made with the dog clan priest that you sicked on our parents?" Those last words bounced all over the huge room and they seemed to return back at the table where the trio sat over and over again.

Sarset broke the silence, she could tell by the long lock of Seti's hair that hung down beside his lowered head that he had no response for Menkaraa. "May I speak for a moment?" Neither man responded. Sarset took that as a yes. "It is quite strange for me to sit here among the two of you. I am a simple farmer's daughter who up until now could not imagine meeting people such as yourselves. I am now perplexed at what is real and what is imagined. I ask myself, Sarset what are these two beautiful men sitting with you? Are they monsters or men whom fate has seduced into her web? I know nothing of the life you two speak of, only that it sounds like a magnificent place you once lived. I hear the pain in Menkaraa's voice; it is familiar to my ear because it is the same sound I heard in my father's voice when I was a little girl. I have only recently known Menkaraa and I know you sir only from the tale he has begun to relate to me. And even though I don't know the whole story yet I must say the two of you need each other more than any two people I have met." "Why do you say such a thing?" Menkaraa probed now standing from his seat and walking from the table.

"Menkaraa", she began, reaching to touch his hand. "This is your brother. I don't know how long the two of you have gone without seeing each other or speaking but he did say he sought you out. Surely you can hear him out and decide on what you think or feel about it. Menkaraa turned back where Seti sat, "I feel nothing for him, he has left misery and sorrow behind every place he has been. I don't know this person who has assaulted my house and my personage. That sits at this table at this moment asking to be heard. He is a memory long forgotten and dead." Menkaraa turned toward the door as if he would leave the room, Seti spoke, and "all you have said is true brother I am a most selfish being I have perpetuated my will endlessly and have not taken any prisoners. I have acted without thought of damage or harm to whomever I have encountered. These things I am guilty of, you stand over me as you always have, the prince of royal blood, whose mother is the queen of all women."

Chapter Twelve

The trio moved in unison through the hall, they had much to prepare and finish before the day brought Ra back into their midst. Bak had spent the nights teaching them about the limitations of this new power. They were eager students; their entourage had increased night after night. When they sat down with their older sons, the discussion was long and odious. Rahotep was firmly against giving the power of immortality to his warrior general brothers. "It would be a mistake father", he began, "to entrust such power to men of war. In a moment you would have dissension in your own house, and the struggle for power will begin at home instead of our enemies." "Are you saying men of war have no honor Ra?" Sesostris roared at him.

"Father if I may speak", Rameses was the cooler head of the two generals, Userkaf and Sesostris. "We are the fodder for any grand ideas thought of in this chamber, we are the first to enforce and be challenged at the word of the king. You send us into lands that hate our customs and laws. We lose the sons and daughters of Kemet in every skirmish and we hear not from our home of birth for months and sometimes years. I ask you father is this the work of men or soldiers who seek to usurp the king our father our blood?"

Menkaure looked at the men seated at the table of Laws. He said to everyone sitting at the table, Bak, Rahotep, Userkaf, Sesostris, Rameses, Sanakht, Khufu, and Ahmose. "I would not be sitting at this table with you men if I didn't trust my life in your hands. I know we all have an opinion of how this should take place, how this new dynasty should perform and where we should begin. I can say only that the men in this room must trust each other without a single doubt of the other's intention. You must master your new gifts and structure your business around its peculiar circumstances. Find the men or women, who will be loyal to you in the day and at night deal accordingly with any treachery. The kingdom of The Setetsenra clan is now and forever, let the weeping of our enemies' women be heard throughout the land. We shall build so great a nation that the sands of time or whim of age shall never swallow it. Let's move forward gentlemen and leave this mortal bickering behind us."

Bak spoke now, "As the god Menkaure has spoken so let it be." One by one each man sitting said, "As god has said." Menkaure's blood surged as he heard the affirmation ring over and over. The vision of Waset was taking form; they would strike against all of their internal enemies within the week. The renegade priest clans would be overrun and only one clan would emerge from the mire of all that pretentious spiritual power. The governors south of Waset and north that were wrestling control of their Nome from the state would be dealt with quickly and without mercy. Khufu the state builder began the new projects with his crews, meeting with them with all the structural details at dusk. They did not know what was different about their prince only that he moved and spoke differently like he was far away always and not near them. The designs of some of these structures were different also; the design was more secretive and peculiar. They noticed that they met as different teams and one team did not know what was going on in the other parts of say a tomb, or library or temple. They did not worry though because their pay was always substantial and on time.

Khufu reveled in his new state as most new creatures; his ability to visualize a structure was accelerated three times from the concept to structure. The face of Waset was literally changing before the people's eyes through his projects alone. Ahmose was meeting with Khufu to discuss the latest libraries he would build, he read faster than before where it took him days to read books, it only took him minutes now and he was devouring every thing in the state libraries. All of these changes moved Kemet to the center stage of the world. Menkaure's family lead the world in development, science, architecture, agriculture, art, philosophy, the king insulated Kemet with these advancements and closed off the borders from intrusions. The armies of Kemet led by the three Blood kings as Userkaf, Rameses and Sesostris came to be known, kept all foreigners out of Kemet while the inauguration of a new nation could take place.

In all of this new surging of the Setetsenra dynasty there was formed a sect that was to be its eternal adversary. They rose up as sudden as the changes in Waset arose, their power fueled by their resolve, they saw Menkaure as a dark shadow, cast furlong over all of Kemet. Their numbers too grew each day like the power of the new dark king. Many of the people did not worship the idea of Menkaure being the living embodiment of the fable god Ausar. The word was seeping out of the palace that some sinister power had overwhelmed the throne. "It is said that the king drinks blood from a golden chalice." The murmuring raced around the table. "Brethren let's not begin and share the tales of unfounded rumors. Let's stick to the business at hand and find just what it is that our king is doing." The men assembled at the table were huddled like conspirators at a coup. The anointed leader of this group was none other than Asret, he whom the king expelled from Kemet.

Asret, looking very weathered. The king's soldiers had escorted him to his house and waited patiently for him at his door. He never came back to the door. He gathered what few humble possessions he owned and slipped out the side door of his hovel. He did not possess a plan, only that he couldn't leave his beloved home, no matter who decreed it. His only crime was to ask a question, he had not rendered Apep's body to shreds. Nor had he sanctioned any of the behaviors of Apep. Menkaure's judgment was not known for mixing with temperance.

Asret loved the Setetsenra family, and wished no harm to any of their house. It appeared that the king had declared strife against all that was religious in Waset and Kemet. He looked around the table at his fellow priests and could not imagine how this disheveled lot would stand up to the sire of Kemet. "We must investigate the rumors of our disturbed king", one priest offered. "Yes Asret you must show us the way, now that the king's house has dealt so foully with Apep." "Hold brethren", Asret began. "We do not know if the house of Setetsenra raised their hands to our master. We cannot begin this investigation with accusations tossed at Kemet's most revered king." A young priest sitting at the table interjected suddenly "What would you have us do then Asret, wait for this revered king to slaughter us all one by one?" Asret did not recognize this young priest he had not seen him in any of the meeting places or temples in Waset. "Your question is premature young one; the king has not killed any priest that I know of." "What of Apep Asret, who rendered him to pieces and left his body at the temple doors?" The other priests entreated, "Yes who did it?" Asret raised his hand for order. "Brethren let us keep our tongues cool and our minds clear. We will seek the answer to all these and other questions that now plague our home. What we will not do is act on unfounded accusations and rumors." The priests all agreed, As Asret has spoken so shall we follow. "What is your plan of action Asret", the priest Nuanti asked. "Yes old friend what is my plan?" Asret said it more as if he was asking the question to himself than simply repeating the request of the priest. "We will begin by gathering true information not lies or tales of madness. Use all your contacts close to the palace and the places the royal family conduct business. We will meet in a neutral location outside of Waset; the king has decreed our sect disband so we will form a new one; one that will not be controlled by a single priest and his ambition." Nuanti interrupted him, "Are you saying Apep's ambition has brought ruin to our sect?" Asret was cautious now, he knew these men were superstitious and had followed the customs laid down by the old high priest very literally. "No Nuanti, I am saying our leader is dead and because our affairs were handled by and through one priest we find ourselves homeless. Let's not find ourselves homeless again."

"Homeless." the repetition of the word came once again from the young priest at the end of the table. "That is a real bone of contention for you Asret?" Asret looked to the priest and being annoyed by his interjections asked "Whom are you young one, what temple have you worshipped in, and why are you among us?" The priests turned to the young one awaiting a response to Asret's questions. The youth bowed his head "no offense to you Asret, I only meant to question your resolve, and you appear hesitant to stand up against the household of Setetsenra. We are besieged by their new plans for Kemet, and they have not invited any religious sects into their meetings. They bark new laws at us like dogs. I wonder if you have the spine and the will to resist." Asret smiled at the youth's brash words, "You of course do, have the spine and will. Gentlemen understand this, if you stand up against a king of this magnitude and popularity, you had better be right and true, for only the gods of Waset will save you if you are wrong. Remember Apep was one of the most powerful priests ever to exist in Kemet, where is he now, call to him can he answer?" The room was silent now and the young priest sat looking at Asret. With a nod he acknowledged that Asret spoke well. "Let us prepare, we are now the Jackal, and Menkaure is the lion. We shall use cunning and wisdom to avoid the jaws of the lion.

"Do we go over the same things again and again Seti? Mother never slighted you, never said a mean or harsh word to you. The queen loved you as her own birth son." "Yes that is well in theory, but the truth of the matter Menkaraa is I could never be the son that inherited the throne. I watched all my brothers look to that throne as being their greatest ascension and I the minor wife son could never look so high." "So those realities brought us to this reality? Is that all brother?" Menkaraa asked with a cavalier tone. "You are not the first person to be scorned by a throne. To see the possibility of never having the people revere you. You made an allegiance with a sworn enemy of the family that loved you because you could not sit on the throne? I once loved you Seti, you were my comfort as a child. I'm no longer a child, and nor do I require your comfort any longer. Leave my house and set your face to see me no longer. I believe the next time I see you it will be as your mortal enemy."

"Menkaraa" Sarset was entreating him. She looked at Seti as the harsh words met his downtrodden ears, and then to Menkaraa, all she could manage was "don't!" Seti rose from his chair, his chin slowly came off his chest until his eyes locked to Menkaraa. He could tell his brother was most sincere in his declaration. He smiled at him, "I will not linger any longer little brother. I have stayed longer than I intended. Know this; you cannot hide from this era, like a rich spoiled child. This age calls to us, the sons of Menkaure can make a difference in this decimated land. We can save this people from their many enemies and teach them to be whole again, to be a nation again. To adhere to the greatness they came from. Turn your back on me Menkaraa, better than you have done it and I forged on, but don't turn your back on your father, his dream and this people; "Not now, not here, not for the carnal pleasure of a peasant girl!"

"Enough" Menkaraa almost screamed the words. Seti raised his palms in surrender. He looked to Sarset "My lady I meant you no slight," he looked back to Menkaraa, "I will see you soon, and I hope we will embrace and not draw swords." With that Seti was gone. "I saw him leave"; Sarset looked puzzled at the empty space he once had occupied. "Where?" She gasped it. They stood for a moment in silence. "I feared that once again I lost my brother."

CHAPTER THIRTEEN

The intelligence gathering was coming along better than Asret and the dog clan had hoped. The only problem was the information was most troubling. Asret had found a meager abode outside of the city of Waset and was browsing the information. He could not believe the report that the king and queen were some kind of night creatures; they were never seen in the light of day. In addition, they appeared to have a cadre of servants that handled their affairs in the daylight time that was fiercely devoted to them only. The accounts said that they did unmentionable things; servants being brought to them and found later with the blood drained from their bodies.

Asret lifted his eyes from the pages of notes. "Blood drained from their bodies," he muttered to himself. He walked over to the small bookshelf containing the books he managed to bring along. Asret ran his finger along the spines until he saw the book he was thinking of *Celestial Hours of the Night.* In it he remembered a tale of Anubis the neter of the dead and resurrection. Asret was beginning to see what was taking place in the noble halls of Waset. Somehow an energy or force had been released on the sire and this force was manipulating him. He needed to know the correlation between the blood and the darkness. "Ah! Here it is" as his finger ran along the page. Anubis the Jackal god of the dead symbolic in its nature let its prey decompose before it ingested it so as to gain the potency of its prey's power, the internal organs were separated and held in a vat of blood eaten separately. This gave Anubis the power over the dead and the ability to reanimate the dead. Asret was excited now; his next question was how to overcome such a power manifested on earth. Surely there is a charm or a spell that can control or even destroy such a manifestation.

Asret delved deeper into the books at his disposal. He was determined to find the answer, and he would save the king, or destroy him whichever was necessary.

Chapter Fourteen

Seti's sudden disappearance left stillness in the room that was like a cool calm after a terrible storm. Menkaraa looked toward Sarset who appeared to be still stunned by Seti's exit. "My dear what do you suppose we do after such a violent interruption like that?" Sarset brought her thoughts back to the now, she mused at Menkaraa's sense of humor and timing. "I think I will eat a little and then retire, I feel Menkaraa that I should go home in the morning. Your life is very complex and whatever it was you might have wanted to say to me, I think, it is now much smaller than what you must now deal with." Menkaraa was slightly taken aback by her words but he gathered himself to respond. Walking over to where she was beginning to eat. He reach for her hand, he intercepted the fork near her mouth.

She looked up at his stoic face, when their eyes met he pulled her up from her seat into his arms. The embrace was awkward at first. Sarset could feel his hard body press her soft flesh and she flinched at first, but suddenly her senses seem to navigate her, they rushed at the feeling of love, and adoration coming from the unknown body touching her. She found herself clutching him as if he would pull away, but Menkaraa was not pulling away he spoke softly in her ear. "I have dreamed of holding you for so many nights now. What I would say to you is no less important than when I first saw you to this night, and I will say it." Menkaraa's pause only magnified the moment. "Sarset I am an unusual creature, I sustain my life whatever kind of life that this is, off of the blood of humans and animals. I have spent hundreds of years trying to rectify my existence. I was at my lowest mental state until that night in the woods when I heard your footfalls. I had not seen a woman as beautiful as you since my childhood. I love you."

The words came soft and quiet, in Sarset's ears. She let them move about in her ears, through her blood, across her flesh, they warmed her and she responded like a woman that had just been told she was to wed the prince. She whispered in his ear "What shall we do about this?" Menkaraa released his embrace and placed both of his hands upon her shoulders he moved her arms length from his body and looked into her eyes. "We shall leave this place; we will travel to a distant land and romance one another, and see where this love will take us."

Sarset's head dropped now, and she slowly moved his hands from her shoulder, "you assume much Menkaraa I have not said I love you."

"But", he began. She cut him off. I am enamored with your life, the tale that you have told me the courage and strength you have shown me. I don't know if I can love a man of your abilities. Yes I find you very attractive and appealing, but what is our future, what of my parents, what of my people our land? You must see Menkaraa before you stepped into my life, I was praying to the ancestors to send a champion to me, to our land. Someone who could stand up to the enemies of Kemet, someone I could love and share a life of rebuilding with. I can't run off and leave my parents and people and land behind. Not even if I love you."

"Sarset I'm not asking you to leave your parents, we can bring them along with us. You will have all that you need to take care of them. I fear for your life here and the life of your parents. If Seti is here the enemies of my father cannot be far behind and they will seek to destroy him and I, and any others that are found to be in league with us. "You are so singular, Menkaraa. This life, this time is not just about you or us" Sarset began. She took his hand and led him back to the chairs at the table. "Now forgive me for being officious, but your brother is not the honorable man that I feel and believe you are. Yet in the space that I observed him he had a great vision and idea. He spoke of his countrymen the people of this land who are being trodden under foot by an enemy that claims all that they stand on. Have you seen the people that your brother has called food? They are a broken lot, all the warriors have been slain or scattered. The women have been forced into servitude like harlots on a quiet dingy street. The children are being sold off in the western part of our beloved continent like cattle and worthless things. Have you paused in all of this time you have had and listened to the heartbeat and voice of the ancestors? You are a man no matter how wronged you have been slighted, with great possibilities and responsibilities. You are both the sun and moon of our people. I have seen you with my own eyes smite the enemy with your sword and your hand. Menkaraa there are few men left with the heart and strength that you manifest so casually. Each day is another day that we will no longer control our own land, our lives, and our destiny." She searched his eyes as the last words reached his ears.

"Okay my dear what would you have me do for this people this land? Bite all their enemies until they go away! Stand before their armies and decimate them with my sword! Humm" he urged. Her answer surprised him "Yes that would be a beginning, a start." Her answer surprised him. Menkara laughed. "Sarset surely you jest? If I interfere with the fate of this land and its people what will be the future interrupted? I could cause a worst thing to come upon the land." "A worst thing has come on the land" she shot back. "We were not meant to have the care taking of this blessed continent wrenched from our grasp and overrun by every foul person that inhabits this planet; we brought forth every civilized thing that man has learned thus far. Will you live isolated while the crime of the century is taking place? Licking your wounds that are centuries old!"

Sarset grasped both of Menkaraa's hands, and implored him "Let go Menkaraa, let go of all the pain and loss. I could be your eyes in the day; with careful planning we could be effective." He stood slowly taking in the words of this woman, a woman he was now in love with. He turned and walked to the door of the dining area, as he opened the door, he turned to look back at her. "I will give this thought Sarset. The morning is drawing to my house. I must rest. We will talk further tonight." Sarset rose. "Wait, I will go see my parents today." "Take a horse from my inventory, the keeper should be there, let him know the master has okayed the borrowing." Sarset reached for his arm, "will you not kiss me good morning?" He looked at her beauty and said, "Will it be a kiss of love or persuasion?" Sarset moved into his arms and this time there was no awkwardness; the kiss was passionate and deep. "You be the judge," she whispered in his ear as they finished. He smiled and turned from her she watched him go off down the hall, a regal being his strides spoke of integrity and bearing. Sarset gathered the dishes she had on the table. She was determined to see her mother and father this day. As she left the kitchen after tidying up she headed for her room, she would dress and seek out this stable and ride to her abode. The mansion, now more familiar had been a great refuge and place of rest. She felt safe as she did as a child under the protective watch of her parents. She remembered her parent's farm was like that before they watched it burn to the ground by the evil ones. As she closed the door to her temporary haven, she looked toward the long hallway to the stairs like a challenge to her destination. "Have no fear Sarset; this house would never harm you." She was not sure if it was her own thought or someone else putting her nervousness at ease. Moving toward the staircase she skipped down the stairs to the front door, looking over her shoulder one last time she said goodbye to the lovely house.

The morning air was fresh and moist, she inhaled and the lungs were ecstatic, "Ahh morning air", there was something special about the first appearance of early morning air, because not many were stirring about, it made the air more personal, yours, "hello sun" she whispered, her face slightly rose to soak the beam of light on her skin. The sounds of distant birds, singing and working brought her out of her exultation, and she looked about where she stood. The estate was much hidden from the rest of the woods; a column of trees rose up in the front so from the grounds looking off into the valley you would not be able to see the city of Karnak. Leading away from the door was a brick laid path that led to the east of the mansion, she was unsure of the destination but felt she had to begin to search somewhere. The grounds were very well kept. Menkaraa must have very loyal people under his employ, she thought. When Sarset neared the edge of the walkway her hunch paid off, in the rear of the side of the house was a medium size structure for all intents and purposes looked like it could be a stable.

"Hello" she called as she approached the building, "is anyone there?" A shadow suddenly moved over her back like something or someone had just blocked the sun. "What can I help you with?" the voice behind her asked. She turned to the voice and was taken aback by the size of the person standing in front of her now. Clearly this man was from the Watusi tribe or Sudanese, every bit six feet ten or seven feet. "Excuse me; I was looking for the keeper of the stable." "That is I," the voice boomed down to her. Sarset tried to place her hand over her brow so as to take the glare of the sun out of her vision and see the tall stranger that stood before her. "Well sir the master told me to tell the keeper that he grants permission for the borrowing of a horse." "I will show you where the horses are; follow me." Sarset could smell the caring of horses now, the straw spewing from the stalls and the gargled sounds of horses moving about peeking their heads out of their places to greet the giant of a man who stood eye to eye to them. He patted the horses on their heads and spoke horse languages to them in an African dialect. "Do you want a mare or a stallion miss?" "As long as it is gentle and friendly either will do," Sarset answered. "I will lend you lady Tye she is a queen of a horse, bred by the Arab conquerors." Sarset looked at the horse, it was beautiful, black shinny coat like it was wet, and her tail in that familiar hoop on the haunches. "Yes" she said, "Tye will do". "I will prepare her miss, and bring her out to you." "Thank you" Sarset replied and began to walk back towards the entrance. "Miss," Sarset turned back to the keeper, "You will find riding clothes in the lockers to the left of the stalls." "Thank you sir." Sarset continued on past the wonderful horses now peeping at their movements.

"Do you know how to ride miss?" Sarset had found nice riding clothes the boots were high and black, the white blouse was feminine and soft and the tan riding pants fit snug on her curvaceous figure. The clothes mimicked the women she saw in town, the English or Dutch she wasn't sure. "I rode quite a bit as a little girl on my father's farm," she replied as the tall keeper approached with the mare. He stops beside her and cupped his hands to give her a boost onto the animal. "Thank you" as she placed her booted foot in his hands and swung her other leg over the animal. The horse moved slightly at the intrusion of her body on its' back, but she pulled the reins and whoaed her to calm. "How do I get to the eastern edge of the woods from Karnak?" The keeper pointed towards the west of the mansion, "go west until you come to the bottom of this hillside, then turn east and as you no longer can see the mansion setting over your shoulder, follow into the thicket until you see the road traveled by many." "Thank you for your hospitality. " Sarset pulled the reins toward the direction, and the sudden gallop of the horse jarred her into her mission.

CHAPTER FIFTEEN

Asret had studied all the Kemetian magic he knew and was taught by his late master Apep. He realized without a personal observation or interaction with whatever had happened to the king he would be unable to draw a clear conclusion as to what to do. I've managed to narrow it down to the forbidden lands, north of our great continent. There is a tale of a people who have been changed by their cruel and harsh environment. They live like animals in caves that are warmed by fire and eat raw flesh and blood. They scour the land to devour it and the people they find on it. Asret thought how could such a people reach Kemet and if such a being did, how did they move about Waset without the palace guards seeing them.

"Asret", Menkaraa began, your scheming leader, and old friend has attempted to dethrone the house of Setetsenra, in his failed attempt he was slain by his comrade. Asret recalled the words of the king, and thought about what the king said. Is it true; was Apep in league with a foreigner? Did this foreigner slay his old friend? Asret gathered his materials. He would speak to his collective of priest about their possible objectives. It was obvious that they would need to prepare and ready themselves for whatever they decided to do. Asret pulled his cowl over his shoulders and closed the door.

The walk to the sanctum was not far, the priest agreed to meet today and he would be ready to explain all he had discovered so far. The door swung open to the room of scheming priest. Their eyes watched Asret as he leaned against the door shutting it and juggling the scrolls and books in his arms. Nuanti stood to help his leader, Asret waved him off. I am fine Nuanti, Asret spoke to his fellow. "Let us begin this meeting and may the God Ptah be with us." The priests in unison said "Amen-Ra."

As Asret placed all of his materials on the huge table that stretched before the priest, he looked around at all of the faces of the men he would join in with this pack against the throne, or for the throne. He was trying to get a sense of where their hearts lied, he knew that Nuanti his faithful friend of many years would stand with him, they were neophytes together as young men coming of age. They studied under the great teachers of their time. "Gentlemen," Asret began, we are gathered here tonight to begin a journey that many of us may not agree on philosophically, spiritually or morally. We are now an outcast to the nation of Kemet. The edict of our sovereign leader makes this meeting an action against the kingdom; we are the few who love Kemet enough to not allow her to sink to barbarism and anarchy." "Yes, yes Asret speaks true," The priest uttered. Asret nodded his head to their approval and continued.

A scourge from the northern lands that was in league with our demised leader Apep has infiltrated our beloved land. The dissension of disapproval raced along the table, Asret raised his arms "gentlemen I will not stand here and argue the point of Apep's intention. What I will say I will say once and never again. Apep our leader for all intents and purposes betrayed the order of this sect, we are men who are chosen by the ancestors to guide and advise on the people's spiritual health. Our commission is not to gain power for individuals in our order or others outside. We are to serve the king and the nation of Kemet."

The words silenced the priests murmuring at the table. Whatever affection the men may have held for Apep, the words of Asret seemed to reach out and dissolve their earlier resolve. "Now," Asret began, "let us get on with the business at hand." One of the priest rose from his seat, "sir may I speak?" Asret nodded his head for him to speak. "Sir I have observed the people beginning to worship Menkaure as the god Ausar. They speak of him as being resurrected as having the power to circumvent death. We have begun to lose our spiritual leadership of the people, if this continues, unchallenged what will be our need in the land?" Asret looked about the room, all of the men sitting waited for his response, and he knew they may not agree, but he gave it to them any way.

"We may have to learn to serve this new god in Kemet if that is what our king has become." The room exploded with disapproval, "never" was mumbled in multiples. Nuanti spoke now, "Asret are we now to be taught by the king on spiritual matters? The priesthood has always taught the kingdom our eyes have led the king; they have always tempered the man in charge of the nation." "I know old friend", Asret began, "and I believe we are about to witness a different order of things. If our king has fallen under the magic of some foul evil that none of us have ever beheld, this could probably change the world, as we understand it."

Menkaraa smiled to himself as he made his way down through the colonnade, he couldn't believe the temerity of Sarset, she truly was an interesting woman. "I'll be your eyes in the day"; he had to admit that was tempting and he felt she would never betray him. Menkara's senses were very keen and acute, and he felt no dishonesty in her words he thought as he entered his sanctuary. Ku growled at his appearance, he seemed pleased at Menkaraa's appearance and also seemed to warn him that day drew near. Menkaraa stopped before the beast for a moment and knelt down to stroke his huge head, looking in the animal's eyes Menkaraa said "Ku I believe she is the one," the lion pulled his head away and walked over to the rest chamber. Menkaraa stood and laughed "You are jealous big fellow, I love you too you will learn to love her as I do, you will see."

Menkaraa could now feel Ra rising in the sky, he ran toward the closed door, jumped, and stretched his hands out like a diver ready to penetrate water and as his fingertips reached the closed door he dematerialized thorough to the other side and in the same moment materialized; he slowed his speed just above his bed and slowly turned over and descended down to his covers and pillows. He was feeling pretty full of himself. Tomorrow would be the beginning of a very different decision for him. Would he take Sarset and Seti up on their offer to change this land? He had not ever thought of the land he fed on, he just fed and grew distance from his humanity. Maybe it was time for him to enter back into the affairs of man and this land. Sarset certainly was worth him exploring the possibility, and she was mesmerizing. He had to be careful, just watching her eat was sensual to him. The vampire is asleep now and at the foot of his bed a small wisp of smoke is rising, it came from underneath his door, and was now filling the room.

CHAPTER SIXTEEN

The horse's breath was all Sarset could hear in the road, as the animal labored at her coaxing. Riding was something she missed; she felt empowered. A beautiful animal such as she was riding most villagers only got to see soldiers or individuals of wealth ride. It drove forward with its mane flagging in the wind and the sound of its hooves striking the road was rhythmic and echoed in the trees. She was getting closer to her home, when suddenly she noticed a stream of smoke rising in the area where she knew her parents were at. She pulled back on the reins and the horse halted its gallop. She rose up in the saddle and made certain it did not appear to be a fire of someone camped out, and it did appear to be in the location of her home. She sat back down and kicked the horse quickly. The animal lurched forward and resumed its gait, only a little more urgently. Sarset tried not to panic; her mother and father were very vulnerable in this land and she hoped that they were safe and in no danger. She tried to ease her mind and thought maybe father is just burning some old shrub. .

As her horse drew near she could see the backs of the foreigners. She slowed her horse and dismounted. They had not seen or heard her approaching, so she pulled the horse into the tree-lined road and hid behind a tree.

"Did you hear that?" The two soldiers turned in the direction of the road behind them. They peered at the empty road and decided it was just an animal in the bush. "You are scared like a child Abdul," they both laughed as they turned back to the spectacle before them. Sarset was not sure if they heard her in the brush, and now her heart began to race. What had them attentive? She was not trying to imagine the worst but a soldier at her home was not a good sign. Beyond Sarset's vision, the thing she feared was taking place. A small regiment of Arab soldiers was holding ground in front of her small cottage. A brutal man was interrogating Sarset's mother and father. He towered over them, kneeled before him on the ground. Sarset's mother held her ailing husband in her arms like a mother would embrace a child to protect them from harm. We know nothing of our daughter's whereabouts, my husband is ill and we have not the strength to keep up with young people. The bearded stranger scowled at the woman's words, "Old woman six of my men are dead, and someone or something has ripped the life out of their carcasses. I am the emir in this place; I will not be ridiculed or challenged." "Sir we speak the truth, our daughter has been gone for a few days and we have not heard from her." "Silence", the commander held his hand open toward the old couple, "you will say no more."

He turned away from them and mounted his horse, pulling the reins of the animal; he barked orders to his men. "Arrest these two, and burn the house to the ground." Sarset's mother screamed, "No, it is all we have left." She pleaded to the man, "have you not destroyed enough of our homes and land, will you not show mercy to even the old? We know nothing of your men and we know not where our daughter is." The emir rode his horse close to the kneeling woman. The horse, uncomfortable at the distance, shuffled and backed up trying to keep a comfortable distance. He restrained the beast and kept close. Looking down on them he growled. "No one showed my men mercy and this land and home is a small price for their lives." He jerked the horse's head away and spit on the ground. He lurched his horse forward and shouted, "Burn it." Suddenly Sarset stepped from behind the wooded covering; she raised her hand and screamed "No". The two soldiers that had missed her initially now spun around to the sound of her voice. The emir looked to her and commanded his men to seize her.

Suddenly all that appeared around those that were acting out this human dance of interaction were interrupted. The woods went dark as if night actually was descending but actually the atmosphere was experiencing a great disturbance. The fabric of the air was crackling and Sarset looked with amazement as six plumes of smoke exploded one after the other. Six tears in the dark, like a rip in the fabric of space as if something were prying it open. The opening increased and she gasped as six figures stepped through the openings of light and suddenly shut back behind their entrance. The dark cowled beings stood still before the emir and his soldiers and Sarset's parents. The emir pulled his horse back around from Sarset and looked at the newly arrived intruders. He rose up upon his horse and spoke "I don't know who you think you are but this is the occupied land of Allah's servant Caliph Omar." The strangers did not move, they did not speak, and looking at them their garments were all black with a large hood. It was impossible to see who or what was under the hood. It was evident they were here to control the situation. As the smoke cleared and the blinding light diminished, you could see their hands covered with symbols that the ancients used to speak of bejeweled down to the thumbs.

They snatched their hoods back revealing the head of the Kemetic jackal god Anubis. The six beings spoke as one voice in unison like a chorus, "Captain your men will cease all action against these people at once." The emir's soldiers took a step back at the sound of their voice and faces, the horses shuddered also, and it was as though they spoke a spell over all that was present. Sarset made her way down to her parents while the foreigners were taken aback by the words. As she neared the perimeter that the beings had put between the soldiers and her parents, two of the beings grabbed her by her arms and held her still. All at once the voice came "you are the one we seek, you have been with the unclean one. You will tell us where he sleeps." Sarset struggled in their embrace; "I don't know what you are talking about. Let me go, let me speak to my mother and father." "The old ones will come too, if you will not tell us what we need to know, then I am sure your parents will help persuade you." "I don't know what you dog things are," the emir shouted from his horse, "but my men and I are not letting you have our prisoners." "Take them." Sarset was suddenly let go by the two who held her arms.

What her parents and her witnessed next only warriors have seen up close. The six figures one after the other stripped out of their dark cloaks. Underneath their covering they wore battle armor. Three of the men had bows, like the mighty Tasheti bowman of the south. The other three held swords of impeccable design. They did not speak another word they just struck in unison. The bowman drew and the arrows' precision twit sound pierced the air, striking the emir and the two soldiers behind them in their throats. The emir gasped in shock at the speed of the assault, he was reaching for the weapon that had invaded his body as he fell from his horse to the ground. The emir's men moved toward the intruders, now cautiously, and Sarset thought she might have seen this before. The three swordsmen handled their swords as nimble as Menkaraa had the first night she had seen him, this was what struck her as familiar. They met the men in stride and clashed swords blade to blade. Three against six seemed to be unfair odds, but it was obvious that the three were trained very well, and quickly they showed how well. The Arabs' large sickle swords were cumbersome and the battle was over in minutes. The sound and flashing of metal was overwhelming as the small contingent of soldiers that once stood before them lay decimated on the ground. As the strangers wiped the blood from their swords and reholstered them, they turned back to Sarset. "You will come with us now," in the same unison one voice one sound.

One appeared to Sarset to be the leader of the six garbed-ones, only because he raised his hand and the horses of the slain soldiers moved towards them as if a rider were sitting upon them. The other five beings helped her parents to their feet and upon the horses, Sarset looked for the horse that she rode in on but could not see the beautiful black mare. The beings now held her horse's bridle straps in their grasp and her mother's horse and her father clutched unto his rider's back. The horses headed toward town moving slowly at first then gathering speed. Sarset looked back over her shoulder, the home she knew grew distant, and men lay slain on the ground. Blood, trampled soil, all of these things would be a testimony of what occurred here today. She could not help but think that her life here was over, done. These beings whatever they were did not seem friendly, and they called Menkaraa the unclean one. She knew she would tell them nothing, and they would probably kill her and her parents too. The wind blowing against her face wiped the single tear from her cheek. Now it too was added to the blood soil evidence.

As the horses approached the opening of the wooded area and followed the road back to the people that lived in the village. Sarset's spirit fell, and she felt the horse's urgings by the being. Their cowls came back over their heads once the shadow of the forest no longer hid their black dog like countenance. What must they look like six robed cowled bodies on horses, two women and an old man holding on for dear life as the horses began a strong gallop, moving past the people in the town that appeared transfixed at the anomalous processional.

The mist that filled the room of Menkaraa was taking on a shape, the figure stood at the foot of the sleeping blood child. The intruder too wore a hooded garment. He looked about the room as if something unusual had brought him to this place. His hooded garment moved to the left, up and then to the right. Finally it stopped at the lying form on the bed. He looked at the sleeping man for a moment, and then he spoke "Wake son of Menkaure, youngest of the Setetsenra clan." The voice appeared loud in the enclosed room.

Menkaraa could hear sound reaching his ears, he was in a deep sleep but something or someone seemed to be calling him, waking him. As his eyes slowly opened he thought a figure stood at the foot of his bed, but he knew no one would dare breech his sleep or his sanctuary. Menkaraa lunged forward at the shadow at the bottom of his bed. The impact of the wall halted his assault; he was more stunned by the idea that he missed the intended target than the fact that the wall was unkind to him. Who could move fast enough to avoid his initial attack? "It is possible for me;" the voice spoke to his question. Menkaraa gathered himself up and turned to see a figure sitting in the chair near his bed. He could not make out the face under the cowl, but he recognized something familiar in his voice. "Yes my prince it is I", as the being spoke the words, he pulled the hood back over his head to reveal the face of Bak.

Menkaraa was stunned he moved uneasily back near the wall. "How is it that you are alive and sitting in my presence?" "I have always been here prince, and I have always been alive. There are things that you need to know and learn, sit, speak with me a moment, I will try to answer your questions." "No, Bak, I am no longer a child that you can snatch in the night. You are my father's friend and confidant, leave my chamber and wait for me in the outer room."

Bak rose from the chair, "I mean you no disrespect my lord. I am the humble servant of Menkaure, but it is he who has charged me to look after you. This I have done faithfully. You are impetuous but still my sire's son." "Look after me what have you done for me Bak? I..." Menkaraa was about to begin a litany of things that he had done for himself. When Bak walked towards the door and appeared to change from human to a lion, a very familiar lion. Menkaraa was stunned, "no not Ku you couldn't possibly." Bak moved to the outer chamber and sat down in a chair facing Menkaraa's sleeping chamber, he waited for the entrance of the prince of Waset.

As if on cue, Menkaraa came through the door behind the late vizier of his father. "Bak how are you able to take the form of my companion, this is a trick I've not seen done by the magicians of our era or this one?" "It is not a trick prince or an illusion, I have been your travel companion Ku the faithful because it is as your father wished." Menkaraa did not know how to take the words coming from the mouth of Bak. He breathed as if he was resolute in hearing the measure of the statement. He walked to his gold laden chair where he had stroked the head of the beast many times, and now the beast he thought was a true confidant, sat across from him in the personage of Bak the grand vizier of ancient Waset. "Where would you wish for me to begin my lord?" Bak said gently as if he was to begin a folktale designed to capture the mind of a small Kemetian child, "Your father, your mother, the war with the dog clan, the betrayal of Seti?" "My mother is she alive?" Menkaraa asked the question rising slightly on the arm of his chair like an eager son needing to know if his hope was not unfounded.

Bak looked to the prince, this you know already. We are a different clan since the attack on your father. The fact that an enemy intended to destroy us has given us an advantage. Menkaraa shot back quickly, "how so, to crawl around in the dark like snakes and reptiles that ambush their prey?" Bak slightly smirked at the castigation of his remark. "You are as melancholy as ever prince, and your tongue is as sharp as a well-kept sword. We are not the beasts that you see yourself as. You have simply traded mortality for immortality. You need to be comfortable in your new gift, and learn to harness the power the ancestors have blessed you with." Menkaraa raised his hand and flailed it back and forth as if he was waving "No, no I don't have to get comfortable with this gift as you call it. This power I neither asked for it nor sought it out." He stood now pointing an accusing finger at Bak and raising his voice slightly, "you, you and my father did this thing to me. And

I've run from it each day of my life. Your ambitious plan and need to forge an everlasting dynasty has destroyed all that I know or have known. What of my mother is she alive or destroyed in this war with my father's enemies?"

The ride was precarious; the jostling of the bodies on the backs of horses being driven by the dog things was unsettling. They appeared to be heading north of Karnak towards the cities being overrun by foreigners, The Arab occupation of the land was no better than the early Greek and Romans. The disappearance of so many clans spoke of the beginnings of marketing of human flesh. Sarset thought, "was this to be her fate and the fate of her parents?" Suddenly the single file horses with riders and occupants turned west, this was not a good sign the great burials were the only things this way. The green of Karnak gave way to dry earth and beyond that sand and dust. The horses slowed and in the distance Sarset could see what looked like a temple of some fashion that the sun was beaming off of. But they would first have to transverse the Aur River. The contrast of the two sides of her homeland was extraordinary, seeing the plush side of the east of Kemet was like beholding a garden in paradise. The west of Kemet was the sand and heat, a land hard for enemies to navigate and home of many dead great kings.

The temple was an odd placement for priest out over the vastness of the wasteland. The jutting colonnades were of ancient design and the horses rode straight towards the archway. The hollow sound of their hooves on the stone resonated that they had arrived. As the group poured into the courtyard of the temple, the familiar towering lotus columns were breathtaking. The colors and Medu Neter inscribed on the stone was mesmerizing to the eyes. The beings all at once dismounted and bowed toward the steps rising along side the statues of Anubis the god of the dead. Sarset looked to where the beings bowed in homage. Standing at the top of the steps at the north end of the open courtyard appeared to be the leader of this band of men, if that was what they were?

Their leader wore the clothing of a priest, but not the priest of this age. His head was shaven and except for ornaments on his arms and fingers his upper body was naked to the sun. A slightly tight linen cloth that came to the top of his knees covered his waist. His feet were bare as if the stone of the floor had spewed him forth. "Rise minions of Anubis; bring our guest forward that I may examine them." The beings rose from their knelt position and in unison removed the dog like masks, now Sarset saw that they were only men masked like children playing games of monsters and demons. They too had their heads shaven; they spoke again in unison "step forward and greet Lord Wepwawet."

"Come closer children", he motioned with an outstretched hand. Sarset held the weight of her father between her mothers and stepped slowly forward. Her parents seemed dazed by the ride and the circumstances that had invaded their lives. She could see that their bodies begged for rest and comfort. "Please sir" Sarset implored, "allow my parents to leave, they are old and not able to endure this hardship." "You do not know me child" the priest spoke down at them. "My fellow priest will give your people rest and nourishment but we can't allow any of you to leave until we find the unclean one." "Sarset's mother with her hand shielding the lowering sun from her vision asked, "Who is this unclean one and what could we possibly know of this individual?" "Speak no more" Wepwawet admonished them. "Take the parents to a holding chamber feed them, allow them to wash. Bring the young woman into the judgment hall and let us reason with her knowledge." He turned from the assemblage and Sarset watched him disappear as if he was sinking much like the days waning sun at their eyes standing in the courtyard.

The priest escorted the elder couple in a separate direction than Sarset; she looked over her shoulder ever so slightly to glimpse her parents for what appeared to be another harsh moment for them. Her mother looked back at her and their eyes spoke in silence that it was going to be all right, at that moment she hung her head in shame for dragging them into the middle of this daymare. This temple appeared to be unlike the sanctuaries in Karnak, it had the hum of business not worship. She saw and heard priest that moved like warriors not servants of Ptah.

They walked up, the men that flanked her, to a great door with deep carvings of ancient symbols and gold handles. "Stand here woman" the priests said in unison. The man to her left stepped forward and opened the large door. He then turned to her, "enter." Sarset stepped forward uneasily at first, and as she eased by the guard and the door she felt the door slam behind her, it startled her at first and then a voice beckoned to her. "Come my dear, step out of the shadow of the door and sit before us." Sarset took a few more steps in the direction of the voice and the light of the room now greeted her. Five priests sat at a large round table. She recognized only the priest that had greeted them in the courtyard. Sarset walked up to the edge of the seat that appeared to be vacant for her and stood. She looked at the men that stared at her and without thought the words just jumped out she said, "What do you want of me?" "We ask you to sit, will you stand and disrespect our request?" "Who are you that you can kidnap my parents and me, and then interrogate me?" One of the other priests at the table spoke "now, young woman mind your tongue and your temperament. You stand before the high council of the Asretian order."

Sarset calmly asked "and who or what is the Asretian order?" Wepwawet spoke now, "you can stand if that is what you choose to do, we will ask the questions here and you will be so kind as to answer them." "And if I don't" Sarset replied. "Then young lady you will have the unfortunate task of becoming the enemy of our order instead of a guest." The priest spoke in an unkind and menacing tone.

CHAPTER SEVENTEEN

"If you would be still but for a moment prince I will tell you what I know". Menkaraa looked at the elder of his childhood, he remembered what his father had taught them as children that the men with power you kept close to you. This vizier of his father was a powerful man and from his unaltered age, a creature like himself. He would listen to this conjurer for now. "My time is short Bak make this quick I have business to attend."

"As you wish" and Bak began to recount his memories, "your mother and father came under attack by a new enemy in Waset. It appeared that the priest that we exiled by the name of Asret was up to much mischief." "Could he have been up to any more mischief than you and my family?" Menkaraa shot back. "True, true", Bak responded, "but we sought to raise a besieged land and keep the enemies of Kemet out of her borders. You and your brother Seti were growing year by year you were being taught by the finest teachers in the land." "These things I know already wizard, tell me how Seti betrayed my father and mother." "Well we knew right away that you were skilled in the sword, and was very good in classes that dealt in art and literature. It was obvious that you were destined to be a scholar if you chose to. Your brother Seti was an expert in the bow, he was crass and arrogant he loved war and confrontation. He read the books of dark arts and magic. He was becoming unmanageable so we had to isolate him from your training facility.

Understand prince, we were growing as a nation proportional to our ability to manipulate our newfound gifts. In a decade we had slain all our border enemies. To the north and west no incursions occurred from foreign feet. We became the envy of the world. Your older brothers Userkaf, Sesostris and Rameses lead the charge against the armies, they became known as the blood kings because the battles that their men finished were scoured with blood. You of course know the other reasons they were named so. Did you know that Userkaf developed a way to peruse his troops in the day and even drink the blood of fallen leaders on the battlefields before his men? You see Ra is at its ebb in the waning hours but yet there is still light but not enough light to pierce through to his skin and the war helmet he crafted. This motivated his men to absolute hysteria to see the great son of Menkaure slay their enemies before all the men and drink his blood. The warriors are strange, prince but needful." Menkaraa was humbled by the new information on his brothers he answered the accusation as if he was a young child, under his breath carried away by the words, "yes, I know. But then we met our strongest test for this thriving nation, the dog clan. An enemy that we had no idea was plotting and waiting for an opportunity to strike and war with us. An enemy within our borders that waited until the blood kings left for explorations in new countries and continents.

"And why did this dog clan attack us Bak?" Bak looked to the young prince's question, his answer was steady and sure, "because power is a strong magnet. Many seek to wield it and control it Menkaraa. The priest saw your father gathering great power to him and the kingdom. Your father was accomplishing this without the sanction or help of any of the religious cults. We never intended to offend any of the religious temples but we did not need their guidance either. This started the purgings, the religious wars. Asret discovered information on our plans and our daily business. I spoke to your father about Seti's steady disgruntled attitude toward his training and his delving into the dark arts. I feared these priests that followed Asret into this alliance to stop Menkaure could sway him. We decided to intervene in Seti's tutelage and bring him into our fold.

The royal guards appeared at his facility and as usual he was engaged in his ill-advised incantations. The guards called to him "Prince Seti you are summoned by Lord Menkaure please follow us." Menkaraa laughed at the image of the palace guards trying to get Seti to follow them anywhere. "What did he do turn them into snakes?" At first, but when I appeared at his chamber he capitulated. He followed reluctantly and as he stepped out of his door I looked at him and then at the snake slithering at our feet. He turned away and threw one hand back toward the floor and a disoriented palace guard reappeared in a fetal position. I believe he mumbled the words it is their true selves. As we stood at the door of your father's study, I said only one thing to Seti. Try to listen to your father prince and weigh his words carefully. He didn't even look at me as he responded," "Bak I am no longer a teen, needing advice from teachers and old men." "With that, Seti grasped the doors by their handles and flung open the doors. Your father sat at the large desk in the center of the room. "Come in Seti, Bak, let us talk and agree together". "I stood which is my accustomed manner in the presence of the King. Seti irreverently flopped down in the handcrafted chairs in your father's study and asked," "Why have you called me father, I was interrupted in the middle of my studies." "Your father was stoic he did not react to Seti's disrespectful tone or gestures. "Seti what is it that you could be studying on a day off from our scholars. He looked back at your father and said sarcastically, "why would the great king of Waset want to know what a lowly son as myself is studying?" "I immediately pointed my finger at Seti and interjected, for him to mind his tongue." Your father raised his hand to stop me from speaking further. Hotep, Bak, let him speak freely. As you wish my lord and I stood back attentive to the verbal spar.

What is it that you think I have done to you son to offend you so? Well let's see Seti began in his obnoxious tone. I've been held prisoner now since I was seventeen years old, cut off from my brothers, treated like a project, punished constantly as a youth, well father am I leaving anything out, because if I am please tell me. Your father sighed deep, "Seti do you have any idea what is going on in this kingdom and how much has changed since we protected you and your younger brothers from these things? Well da-dee seeing how it appears you haven't aged a bit and I don't see you except in the evenings and according to my books I would say you was some kind of creature of the night. Maybe even Ausar himself as the rumors purport.

Your Father looked to me and his eyes bade me to leave, I bowed and said to the king of Waset I take my leave my lord I will return at your word. I left the room but as it is my duty I kept an eye on the King. In my sanctum I possess the Wadjet of Kemet the all seeing eye of Heru. I waved my hand across the orb of the eye and the room where your brother and father spoke in came into view. Our king had stepped back to the side of the desk and look to Seti again. "Seti, I will tell you this, you have become a great concern to me of late. You leave your chambers without permission and you are gone for hours, you respect no authority that I have laid to your charge. This is not the behavior of a son of the king. "Father I am not a child any longer, do you expect me to be held like a child until I am an old man?" "Not until you are an old man but until you are old enough." "I am old enough; I am twenty four years old I have trained and read in captivity for seven long years now. You treat me as an enemy of the state." "Enough Seti", Menkaure interjected. "No, no father I have not said enough, I am one of nine sons you have and I am not out of the lineage of the grand wife. Let's see that means I inherit nothing, I am as insignificant as a fly."

The king stood and stepped towards Seti, Seti looked back from where he sat, "what, will you strike me now for speaking to the king in such a tone?" Your father told him to stand, Seti was about to speak again and your father spoke more aggressively this time "Stand son of Menkaure and say not another word from your insolent tongue." Seti stood a little less confident than the moment ago. "I will give you what you seek my son, you say you are grown and able to stand in this kingdom, you have read your books and studied with the scribes and the warriors." Menkaure turned slowly away from Seti for a moment while still talking to him; "well in your rich tutelage did you ever come across this?" He turned back toward Seti and his great canine teeth were bared; Seti was frozen but the King did not wait for a response from him. He pulled him into his embrace and sunk his teeth into his neck.

"No more Bak, this is a tale I vaguely can see in my dreams." "They are not dreams my prince or visions of a creature gone mad. You see what is a part of every creature that shares the blood exchange; images of the life of the sire. You see pieces of your father's life because he exchanged blood with you."

Sarset steeled herself to the stares of the five priests staring menacingly down at her. She had determined in her mind that she would tell them nothing of Menkaraa, "I don't believe that priest have enemies, save demons or the devil himself" she softly responded to the statement they last spoke. Wepwawet spoke again "we have not determined you to be an enemy yet, are you implying that is the case?" Sarset stepped closer to the open chair and looked at the five priests; they were smug sitting in their clothing reserved for the emissaries of god. Looking at her as if she was some blight on the earth. She could hear one whisper to the other "she has been with the unclean thing I smell his stink on her." This forced a response from her observing mind. "I will answer your questions and you will release my mother and father and me." In unison they responded "yes" like hungry hyenas.

She pulled the chair back and sat down. "Ask away, what is it that you seek to know that I can't possibly tell you?" "Do you know of a thing called Menkaraa?" Sarset answered "a thing, what kind of thing and what is a Menkaraa?" Wepwawet jumped to his feet "you would play with us child, we know you have been with the beast and we know you know its nature." Sarset calmly responded, "then why this charade, why are you pretending to ask me questions you claim you already know? I tell you I know nothing of this thing you seek and I feel that if I did after the rude way you have spoken to me and whispered to each other, if I knew something I would not breathe a word to the likes of you five." "You my dear may regret such words spewing from your mouth." One of the other priests stood now, "what, has this thing beguiled you has he swayed you with his charm and beauty? Your eyes deceive you my dear he is not what he appears to your senses. We are the cleansers of these foul things and you are but a village girl mesmerized by thousand of years of charm. Do you think such a thing has reached out to a young innocent being this first time? You are but one of hundreds he has swayed." "I see", Sarset began; "you don't need me you five know all and have seen all. I will take my parents and be returning to Karnak." "We have ways of loosening your tongue child, this is a serious war and if you stand between us and evil you will be harmed in the exchange."

Sarset stood now, and looked at all the men in the room. "You call this a war, scouring the earth for one man while a nation is at your doorstep. Have you seen the missing people of our city being taken to the lands of strangers never to be seen again while you were at war with this one thing or man? Evil is not this war you have with this Menkaraa. You are evil, you and this whole clan of yours that has its entire energy focused on one thing while the real evil takes root and rips our land apart." "These things are not our concern, and you have said quite enough. Guards take her to the hall of questions; we will take no further questions from her here."

The men entered and took Sarset by her arms; "Wait, I will tell you this." The priests looked eagerly to her subjugation, "Ahh yes my dear speak." She began "Menkaraa"; they waited with bated breath "yes. He is where?" "Menkaraa will be here, and he will eat each of your miserable hearts when he sees you." "Take her, take her, torture her, let her lips speak only what we need to hear" they covered their ears as she was drug out shouting back to them "he will come he will come and he will eat all of you."

Menkaraa regained his composure, "Bak I have business; I need to know only one other thing from you." Bak stood; he looked to Menkaraa and spoke to him as a father would his only child. "You are too quick to judge son of Menkaure, let not your blood rush through you before you think. The things I have just told you they are for your edification. I have guarded you these many years and watched you struggle with these skills. You need a true mentor who can help you be at peace and hone your gift." Menkaraa had his head lowered as he listened to the words coming form his late father's grand vizier. "And who would this guru be Bak? Certainly you don't entertain yourself as this self-appointed guide; you who have deceived me these many years as an animal companion that I grew to trust and love."

"But these are things you need to know and understand, because we are animations of life. In this dimension we are a different form, we are able to take on a corporal appearance but in many ways we are not corporeal at all. We are able to manipulate the cellular structure of this body. I did not deceive you; I did what I have been born to do, look after the life of the Setetsenra clan." Bak said it as if he was yielding to a greater power than himself. "I hear you Bak, but how has your duty to my family faired so far, is my father or mother alive, are my brothers still on this planet to speak to me like a time long gone?" He waited for a response from the elder. Bak's eyes pierced through his. "Yes". Menkaraa's mouth fell open. "How, where?"?"

Sarset could not tell where the guards were bearing her off to but she steeled herself for the worst, she implored the men to let her parents go, they were unable to do any harm to them. Her pleas fell on deaf ears. Suddenly the air around them began to crackle and Sarset looked at the space around her, it seemed to open the way the eyelid raises when it is shut and closed on an eyeball. She felt her stomach pitch and twist kind of like just before you vomit. Everything went dark and just as suddenly as darkness there was light and she felt herself falling into the light. The popping of atmosphere allowed her to know that she was in another place removed from the temple and on her knees her stomach gave up resisting and the smell of putrid food permeated the floor. "Ahh pick her up and place her in the restraining chair." The voice was unfamiliar but its sound was authoritative and forceful.

As Sarset was trying to gain her balance and visually try to see where she was, a sudden smack across her face greeted her slamming her into the chair. "Maa ismuk" (what is your name?) Sarset's head jolted in the opposite direction of the voice of her assailant. His dialect was Arabic but she hadn't quite adjusted to the room; it smelled of blood and human feces, sweat of tortured and persuaded human life. The blood trickling down her mouth instinctively caused her to spit in the face of her assailant. She saw him now like all the foreigners that milled about in Karnak; he wore his people's nomadic garb head wrapped and full beard. He just wiped the mix of blood and spittle through his beard. Leaning forward in Sarset's face he said "that's it girl, I like to get my work all over me it gives me a sense of accomplishment after a day's good work. You will do good to save your strength; I am told that you have much to tell us and little time to speak."

The men who brought Sarset to the inhuman place of pain, spoke to the keeper. "Our master wants the answers no later than the next day at this hour." "Tell your people I will do my best." They responded, "if it gets the desired information that will be sufficient for him." With the men huddled behind the chair she was strapped in, Sarset could not see them leave but she heard the familiar sound now of space tearing open and she knew they were gone. She braced herself now and thought only of her mother and father, who would care for them and protect them from such an evil that now surrounded their homeland?

The fiendish man moved towards her line of vision again, in front of him was a table that held items she could not make out because of his back hiding a clear view of them. He was humming a little ditty like a child caressing its favorite toy. He would lift an item and Sarset would catch a glimpse of strange misshapen objects, items she had never seen before but she was sure this place of evil was familiar with. He would shake his head and pick up another one. She cursed at him because she knew this was his way of beginning the inevitable assault, "you dirty thing you will not break me and I will tell you nothing." He didn't even answer her; he continued to place the things he intended to use and continued the laughter and conversation with himself. "Yes, yes these will do, let us begin" and slowly he turned toward Sarset with a probe instrument that was not meant to examine a person. Sarset pulled at her restraints flinging curse words and expletives at him. He stopped in front of her appearing shocked and hurt. "My what a powerful little voice you have, let's stop that" and as if he had come up with a great idea, he pulled a piece of cloth from his pocket and forced it into her mouth, muffled sound was all that returned in the room.

The inn was crowded; the mix of natives and the strangers passing through the area was now familiar. There were well-lit areas where people drank and laughed and made deals of the flesh with each other. And there were dark areas where men huddled and planned mischief or just sat alone. In a remote corner of such a dark spot sat Seti, cowl covering his head, making it difficult in this low light to make out his features. The only reason anyone could see that there was a person at the table was the bright red color of the lining of his hooded night cowl. He never wanted to be so inconspicuous when he hunted. He enjoyed the fear of a stranger in an unusual attracting color like this coat looking as if they are trying not be noticed. The waitress stepped over to his table and asked if there was something she could bring him. Seti did not lean forward out of the dark, he let his voice just project out to her, the way the cold wind speaks when you are out in the street alone and it causes you to shudder suddenly. He was pleased it had the same effect when the woman heard, "yes a cold beer thank you."

He scanned the room, and the conversations he perused were nothing new, the young man wanted to have his way with the young lady that was snuggled close to him. The women trying to bargain with the strangers resented them, but needed the money to take care of what was left of their families. He stopped the cruising of minds. When he caught an unfamiliar thought, —torture, Seti found this interesting. He looked for the source of the word. Ahh there, he leaned forward out of the dark of the room and his eyes fixed on two men, drinking and speaking in low whispers. They looked like a general's lowly guards. He pulled his cowl slightly back so that his ear could catch the sound even over this noise of people. "He will kill her; she did not look like the type that would speak." "He is a master at pain she will speak before she dies", the other responded as he tilted the glass to his mouth. "We should get back before he notices we are gone." "One more" the other implored, "he enjoys his work too much to concern himself with our whereabouts besides we are but a stone's throw from his door."

"Hmm interesting," Seti thought, I might keep my eye on these two but they are certainly not the meal I seek tonight. The waitress placed the glass at his table; he touched her hand as she set the beer before him. You my dear are another story "what time are you finished here tonight?" His touch was cold but the woman still answered him "in a few minutes what do you have in mind?" Seti smiled to himself, "oh a drink a meal you know something intimate just you and I."

Menkaraa fell back in his chair. Bak had assaulted him with his tale of Seti and his mother and father alive; he seemed to be able to only mutter his speech. Bak moved over to the prince and placed his hand on the shoulder of his dejected charge. "Don't try to manage this all in an instance Menkaraa, your father and mother have been safely hid from their enemies." Menkaraa could no longer hear the words of Bak; he was hearing the faint sound of his name being called in his mind. He muttered mother, father but he realized that it was not their voice that was intruding in his mind. The voice was familiar and urgent. His eyes widen suddenly he abruptly brushed Bak's hand from his shoulder, Bak did not get a chance to even see or ask where Menkaraa was headed. Menkaraa was moving as fast as a creature of his ability was able to move, his feet were not even touching the ground, the atmosphere supported his lunging forward through the woods. He stopped only for his sword; he could change into his battle gear, as he got closer to his destination. In his mind, if the voice that is tugging at his psyche is who he thinks it is and they are in the danger he feels, some one or something is about to feel the wrath of an unforgiving warrior.

CHAPTER EIGHTEEN

The alley caught the body of the woman, her eyes were open but lifeless; she seemed surprised but resolved in her face. Seti pleasured the warmth of the meal, he had feasted on many blood types and the blood of women and royals was the most satisfying to his being. He dropped the body so frivolously because as he was swooning in the moment and the girl's blood was rushing to his organs he heard the fools at the inn passing and his interest was piqued again. He followed them, as only he knew how, mixing with the night shadows and the slow mist of night air. He watched them take up their station at a stone house that like most of these buildings in this overcrowded city appeared at first glance to be normal dwellings of simple people. The sound of screaming was reaching his ear, faint but just enough for his highly tuned senses. He smirked to himself. His bow was under his cowl. He would look into this because the torture of someone this closely guarded intrigued his dark side. The bow was forged out of metal not wood; his strength was capable of drawing the line it was strung with. His arrows were made of gold tips like that of his ancestors who were called the people of the bow. Seti pulled the end of the arrow and line close to his ear, seeing a target was instantaneous for him; his eyes were like the falcon of Kemet true and clear. The phiss sound of the arrow was all that could be heard as it left the bow and as quick as the first the second arrow was strung and fired reaching its target and felling both men standing at the door of the house.

He walked over to where they had fallen and laughed as he thought the two had seen the "arrow" of their ways. He grabbed them by the tuff of their turbans and dragged them into the dwelling; closing the door he could smell old and fresh blood, whoever was the owner of this place took much pleasure in human suffering. Not something he was not familiar with. He walked across the open patio of the house and as he got to the opening way of the steps that seemed to lead down to the interior of the house, he was even surprised at what his eyes saw. Strung up and fully exposed was his brother's guest: the lovely woman Sarset, her body bruised and bleeding. Her head had fallen down unto her chest and she appeared lifeless. The fool who would do such a thing was standing with his back to him looking at his work as if he had done some great artistic rendering.

Seti drew his bow and the arrow struck the tormentor so hard that it exploded like a piece of fruit. He cut Sarset down; she fell into his arms and he could feel her heart beating against his chest. She murmured "Men...Menkaraa," He snatched a cloth draped over a table in the chamber and wrapped her and ascended the stairs with her in his arms. The openness of the court of the house to the night sky as he reached the top of the stairs was like walking out into the vastness of space. He set her down, she was trying to speak but blood and gurgling was all that was coming out. Seti wiped the blood from her mouth trying to comfort her "You will be alright my lady, be still." She coughed and looked at Seti. Her delirium was easing but she had to tell him before it was too late. "Tell"...coughing of blood followed, "Menkaraa I love him." She tried to catch her hasting breath "tell him I told them nothing." Seti tried to quite her. "Be still, conserve your strength." She shook her head "no it's too late." Tears welled and fell at the corner of her eyes "Convince him Seti to help this people to..." Seti could not let her die. He knew Menkaraa would blame him. He thought the only thing he could do was to deliver her the kiss, but the loss of blood seemed too much already; but he could think of nothing else that had the possibility of saving her. He drew her up to his mouth and felt the blood come to his throat. Her body seemed to understand, and she in her last act, yielded herself to him, almost, pulling his head into her neck as to hasten the act. As the blood surged through his body, he felt the intense pleasure of the moment, and pulled her lifeless body closer to his as if to share their one and last intimate moment together.

Menkaraa was now airborne, the rest of the journey toward the town where he felt the cry of help coming from. He moved toward the opening of a dwelling and looking down he saw his greatest fear "No!!!" he screamed. Below him he could see Seti and Sarset embraced in his arms and looking lifeless. He dropped from the sky like a great stone He struck Seti away from her limp body. He brushed her hair out of her face and spoke lovingly in hear ear "no, no my love, my love what has he done, what has this evil thing done to you?" He pulled away to see her neck punctured and the life that once was here and growing was gone. He kissed her once more on her lips and laid her dead lifeless body on the cold stone. His back was to Seti who was trying to wipe his mouth and regain his feet after Menkaraa's assault from the air. He spoke to Menkaraa's back "It is not what you think brother." "Say nothing Seti. I should have known you would find a way to injure me and cause me misery like I have never felt before." Menkaraa drew his sword sheath in its hilt strapped across his back and turned at the same time to face Seti. I will not fight you brother you mis...Enough Seti, draw your weapon or I will cut you asunder where you stand." Seti could see that Menkaraa would not be reasoned with. He drew his bow and aimed it at his brother. Menkaraa grasped his sword in both of his hands and roared like a large lion protecting his pride......

ABOUT THE AUTHOR

Khpra Senwosret is a 47 yr old native of Baltimore Md. Married, father of two. He presently lives in Pennsylvania with his wife and three stepsons.. Where he continues to write intriguing stories of love,war and nationalism. This is his first published work .He holds a masters degree in life experience and teaches the ancient lost art of kung-fu.Khpra just wants to write the stories that never get written or are written with jaded memory and prejudice. His writing flow reminds you of tales told long ago by griots and scribes." When I read a book I want to be able to see the characters,smell the scenery, experience the pain and joy". Mentor,scholar, philosopher, sifu, husband, father, and writer. Khpra wants you to know that this work is only the beginning of what he wants to offer you the reader.

Made in the USA
Monee, IL
02 August 2022

10781211R00121